Fargo palmed out his .44 as a bullet buzzed past his right ear. Glass shattered behind him, but he didn't look to see what had happened. A second bullet took off his hat as he triggered a shot of his own.

A crimson stain bloomed on the chest of the man who'd played the piano, or tried to, and he fell backward onto the instrument, making a discordant noise as he hit the keys. It sounded little worse than his attempt at playing. His blood stained the ivory keys.

The second man fired again, and Fargo felt the bullet tug at the left arm of his buckskins. He pulled the trigger of the .44 twice, and the man dropped his pistol. His fingers went to his throat, but they couldn't stop the blood that pumped out. He toppled over and fell across the man who was already on the floor.

THE TRAILSMAN

#346

ARKANSAS AMBUSH

by

Jon Sharpe

A SIGNET BOOK

SIGNET
Published by New American Library, a division of
Penguin Group (USA) Inc., 375 Hudson Street,
New York, New York 10014, USA
Penguin Group (Canada), 90 Eglinton Avenue East, Suite 700, Toronto,
Ontario M4P 2Y3, Canada (a division of Pearson Penguin Canada Inc.)
Penguin Books Ltd., 80 Strand, London WC2R 0RL, England
Penguin Ireland, 25 St. Stephen's Green, Dublin 2,
Ireland (a division of Penguin Books Ltd.)
Penguin Group (Australia), 250 Camberwell Road, Camberwell, Victoria 3124,
Australia (a division of Pearson Australia Group Pty. Ltd.)
Penguin Books India Pvt. Ltd., 11 Community Centre, Panchsheel Park,
New Delhi - 110 017, India
Penguin Group (NZ), 67 Apollo Drive, Rosedale, North Shore 0632,
New Zealand (a division of Pearson New Zealand Ltd.)
Penguin Books (South Africa) (Pty.) Ltd., 24 Sturdee Avenue,
Rosebank, Johannesburg 2196, South Africa

Penguin Books Ltd., Registered Offices:
80 Strand, London WC2R 0RL, England

First published by Signet, an imprint of New American Library,
a division of Penguin Group (USA) Inc.

First Printing, August 2010
10 9 8 7 6 5 4 3 2 1

The first chapter of this book previously appeared in *South Pass Snake Pit*, the
three hundred forty-fifth volume in this series.

Copyright © Penguin Group (USA) Inc., 2010
All rights reserved

The Trailsman

Beginnings . . . they bend the tree and they mark the man. Skye Fargo was born when he was eighteen. Terror was his midwife, vengeance his first cry. Killing spawned Skye Fargo, ruthless, cold-blooded murder. Out of the acrid smoke of gunpowder still hanging in the air, he rose, cried out a promise never forgotten.

The Trailsman they began to call him all across the West: searcher, scout, hunter, the man who could see where others only looked, his skills for hire but not his soul, the man who lived each day to the fullest, yet trailed each tomorrow. Skye Fargo, the Trailsman, the seeker who could take the wildness of a land and the wanting of a woman and make them his own.

Arkansas, 1860—where the Trailsman finds himself in hot water in more ways than one.

1

Skye Fargo, the man some called the Trailsman, didn't have trails or tracking on his mind. As his magnificent black-and-white Ovaro stallion picked its way through the towering pines, Fargo thought about Angelique Leblanc with her tumbling black hair, her startling blue eyes, and her other assets, which were considerable.

The big man in buckskins grinned. If he kept this up, he'd be writing poems about her.

Angelique was the kind of woman who could turn a man's thinking in that direction, all right, but before Fargo had a chance to go any further with his imaginings, he heard gunshots. His lake blue eyes narrowed as the heavy boom of a Henry rifle like the one Fargo himself carried was followed by a volley of shots that sounded like they came from a revolver, maybe a couple of revolvers. The Henry boomed twice more, and then it was quiet.

A lot quieter than it had been, in fact. All the sounds of the woods had stopped. No squirrels chattered; no birds sang. Even the humming of the insects died away.

Fargo leaned back in the saddle. The ruckus was none of his business. He told himself to ignore it and keep on riding. He had an appointment with Angelique in Hot

Springs, and he wasn't going to let anything keep him from it.

A rifle crash broke the silence. Pistol shots echoed it.

The Ovaro stopped, its ears perked.

"Damn," Fargo said. "Somebody's in trouble for sure."

It wasn't Fargo's trouble, but trouble, anybody's trouble, always seemed to call to him. He tugged the reins to the left and urged the Ovaro in the direction of the shots.

After Fargo had ridden about a quarter of a mile, the trees thinned out and the forest opened onto a wide clearing. Across the clearing rose a wooded hill.

On Fargo's side of the clearing, a man hunkered down behind a deadfall. His horse lay in the clearing, not far away. As Fargo sat and watched, a bullet from the rifle knocked a big chunk of wood from the deadfall. The man rose up and fired a couple of pistol shots in the direction of the rifle, then dropped back down as pistol shots came from the hill.

The pistols weren't about to do any damage, Fargo thought. The range was just too great. The rifle was the only thing to worry about.

Fargo couldn't tell exactly where the shots had come from. The shooters, and there must have been at least two of them, were concealed in the trees on the hill.

It still wasn't Fargo's fight, but he didn't like the uneven odds, and he didn't like it that a man's horse had been shot. He scratched his dark, short-trimmed beard.

More shots shattered the quiet, and Fargo slid off the Ovaro, looped the reins around a tree branch, and slipped his Henry out of its saddle sheath. He could stay in the concealment of the trees until he was about twenty yards from the deadfall, so he decided to get a closer look at the proceedings.

He made his way forward. There was no danger that he'd be heard. He could move through the woods as quietly as a panther, and the man was concentrating on the people on the hill. He wasn't likely to think anybody'd be coming up behind him.

Fargo stopped when he came to the last of the trees and stood behind the thickest one.

"Don't turn around," he said in a normal voice.

Fargo saw the man's shoulders tighten, but he didn't turn. That showed good sense.

"Who the hell are you?" the man said without looking in Fargo's direction. He didn't raise his voice any more than Fargo had.

"Just somebody passing by," Fargo said. "Somebody who's not gonna shoot you in the back. What's going on here?"

"Damned if I know."

The man was about to say more, but the rifle thundered twice from the trees across the clearing. Chunks of wood flew off the deadfall. This time the man didn't return fire.

"Somebody must not like you," Fargo said when it was quiet again.

"Bastards shot my horse. I don't think they meant to, though. I think they meant to shoot me."

"Looks that way," Fargo said. "You got any idea why?"

"Hell, no. Didn't I just say that?"

Fargo didn't blame the man for being mad. Now that he could see him better, Fargo could tell he was young. Probably inexperienced, too, else he wouldn't have been wasting his bullets shooting at people he couldn't see.

"I was on the way to Hot Springs," the man said. "I'm looking for my pa. When I came out of the trees into the clearing, that's when the shooting started."

3

Could be robbers, Fargo thought. Plenty of them in the territory.

"Who are you, anyway?" the man said. "Some damn vulture come to pick on the leavings?"

"Like I said, just passing by. I'm on my way to Hot Springs, too."

"It's a popular place. You gonna help me out or just stand back there and jaw at me?"

"You sit tight, and I'll see what I can do," Fargo said. He faded back into the trees.

Fargo stopped at the Ovaro and slid the Henry back into the saddle boot. He patted the horse on the neck and started circling through the woods. If the man hidden at the deadfall wasn't expecting anybody to come up at his back, then the men shooting at him likely weren't thinking about anything like that, either. All Fargo had to do was get behind them by taking the long way around.

He didn't think there was any rush. The ambushers couldn't shoot through the trunk of the fallen tree, but Fargo didn't think they'd leave. They wouldn't want the man to get away.

As if to prove the truth of what Fargo was thinking, more rifle shots rattled the air to keep the man pinned down. Fargo didn't hear any answering fire. The youngster wasn't wasting his ammunition anymore.

Fargo circled the clearing and went well up into the trees opposite the deadfall. He wanted to be sure he was behind the men with the rifle. When he thought he'd gone far enough, he stopped.

It was early fall so it was warm in the trees, but not hot. It was early enough that the leaves hadn't started falling. The morning sun filtered down through the trees and patterned the ground. The birds and squirrels were making a racket again, having gotten used to the shooting.

Fargo knew he was close to where he wanted to be,

but he didn't know exactly where the shooters were located, so he'd have to wait until they made some noise. He'd learned patience long ago, and he had time to wait rather than blunder into anything. He sat down at the base of a tree, leaned back, and pulled his hat down over his eyes. He hadn't quite dozed off when he heard shots.

Fargo sat up straight to listen. The shots came from in front of him and a little to his right. He hadn't been far off in his reckoning. He stood up and started to walk.

After a while he could hear someone talking. He made his way a little closer. Two horses were tied to a low tree limb. Two men lay on the ground nearby, a low rise in front of them. They had a good view of the deadfall and the dead horse, but that was about all. The man hidden there was keeping well out of sight.

Fargo loosened his big .44 in its holster. He didn't want to show it and start a shooting match unless he had to. The men in front of him started to talk, and Fargo froze where he stood.

"He ain't taken a shot at us in a good half hour or more," one of the men said. He wore a floppy brimmed hat, dirty pants, and a sweat-stained blue shirt. A Henry rifle lay beside him. "I say he's dead."

"I don't know why the hell you'd think any such of a thing." The second man was dressed like the first, but his clothes were cleaner and his hat was in better shape. "He wasn't dead the last time he poked his head up, and you damn sure didn't hit him with that Henry of yours."

"Hell, Brady, he coulda been hit when the horse fell. Could be why it fell."

"Wasn't hurt a bit, Paulie. He ran for that deadfall like his pants was on fire."

"Might've bled to death."

"If you think so, why don't you go have a look?"

5

"Why don't you?"

"I ain't the one that missed him and shot his horse."

Paulie hit the ground with his fist. "Damn it, I knew you'd say that. Wasn't my fault. The damn horse stumbled."

"That ain't the way I saw it. Horse didn't stumble till you shot it."

"Well, it don't matter how you saw it. One of us better go check on him. If we don't kill him, we don't get paid."

That was all Fargo needed to hear. The men weren't robbers. They'd been hired to kill the downed rider for some reason. Fargo didn't hold with that kind of doings. He pulled his pistol.

"You two fellas keep your hands empty and roll over," he said.

The two men looked at each other and then over their shoulders at Fargo.

"What if we don't?" Brady said.

He didn't sound a bit scared. That wasn't a good sign. When you have the drop on a man, he ought to be at least a little worried.

"I guess I'll have to shoot you in the back," Fargo said. He motioned with the pistol. "Now roll over like I told you."

The men looked at each other again and shrugged. Then they rolled over on their backs.

"Now sit up," Fargo said.

They did as he said, and Fargo told them to put their pistols on the ground by their feet. They looked at each other again.

"Do it," Fargo said.

They both set their guns on the ground next to their feet, but still within easy reach.

"Now kick 'em away from you," Fargo said.

They did that, too, but as they did it, Paulie snapped forward quick as a hungry mountain lion and lunged at him. Fargo slashed the side of his head with the .44, but Paulie still managed to get a hand on Fargo's boot and give it a jerk before falling to the side.

Fargo stumbled backward a step, and Brady jumped to his feet. In the same motion, he jerked off his hat and threw it in Fargo's face. The Trailsman brushed the hat aside just as Brady charged into him and slammed his head into Fargo's stomach.

Had Fargo been prepared for the blow, he could have shrugged it off, but he was caught off guard. He fell back, and Brady landed heavily on him. He grabbed Fargo's wrist and slammed it against a rock. Fargo dropped the .44, and Brady grabbed it.

Fargo caught a handful of Brady's hair and yanked his head hard to the left. Brady fell off Fargo, but he held on to the pistol.

Fargo jumped up before Brady could get off a shot and kicked him in the face, smashing his lips and sending a tooth flying.

Brady dropped the pistol and put his hands to his ruined face. He didn't make a sound, but his shoulders shook as if he might be crying.

Paulie scrabbled across the rocky ground and reached for the pistol. Fargo stomped his hand and felt bones give beneath his boot heel.

Paulie screamed, and Fargo kicked him in the side of the head. He stopped screaming.

Fargo picked up his pistol and brushed off the dirt and pine needles it had accumulated.

"You two are mighty frisky," he said. "I hope you're not going to try anything else like that. I'd hate to have to kill you."

That wasn't strictly true, but Fargo didn't like setting

7

himself up as judge and jury. There still might be more to what was going on here than he knew about.

"You don't have to kill us," Brady said. He was a little hard to understand because of his smashed mouth. "Leave us be and we'll just ride out of here."

That sounded all right to Fargo, but there was one little catch.

"You can leave," Fargo said, "but your guns stay here."

"Damn it, I need that Henry," Paulie said.

"You should've thought of that before you tried bushwhacking somebody with it."

"Maybe you got a point," Paulie said. He struggled to his feet, cradling his hurt hand in the crook of his elbow. "I couldn't shoot it anyway. I think you broke ever' damn bone in my hand."

If he was expecting an apology, he didn't get one.

"Can I at least get my hat?" he said.

"I'll do that for you," Fargo said.

He walked over to where the hat lay, picked it up, and tossed it to Paulie, who reached for it but appeared unable to grasp it with his injured hand. He bent down for it, and Fargo saw too late that one of the pistols was nearby.

Paulie was nothing if not game. He snapped up the pistol with his left hand and tried to trigger a shot.

He didn't even get his finger into the trigger guard before two bullets from Fargo's .44 hit him dead center in his chest.

Fargo turned through drifting gun smoke and saw Brady rolling toward his own pistol. Brady wrapped his fingers around the gun butt and twitched his arm around.

Fargo shot him in the head. Brady's head snapped to the side. He flopped over, firing his pistol even though he didn't know it. He was already dead when the bullet plowed the ground far away from where the Trailsman stood.

Gun smoke stung Fargo's nose, and he waved it away from his face. The two men lay still. It was too bad he'd had to kill them, but they didn't seem inclined to give up. They must've needed the money they were to get for killing the man they'd ambushed. They weren't cowardly, and there wasn't any quit in them. Fargo had to give them credit for that.

Or maybe he didn't. Maybe they were more scared of somebody else than they were of Fargo. If so, that somebody must be really scary. It was something to think about.

The Trailsman holstered his .44 and started across the clearing to let the man know he didn't have to worry any more about being shot.

The man's name was Dave Harragan, and once Fargo saw him close up, he realized Harragan wasn't much more than a kid, really, probably not more than twenty. He was more than a little shaken when he and Fargo looked down at the bodies of the two men Fargo had killed.

"You okay?" Fargo said, seeing that Dave's skin had taken on an unhealthy greenish tinge.

"Yeah," Dave said. He clamped his mouth shut and took deep breaths through his nose.

"We can't just leave them here," Fargo said, nodding at the bodies. "We'll either have to bury them or take them with us."

Dave nodded in agreement, but Fargo could tell he wasn't happy about it.

"Hasn't rained in a good while," Fargo continued. "Ground's hard, wouldn't be easy digging."

Dave nodded again.

"We'd best put 'em on their horses, and take 'em into town." Fargo said.

This time Dave didn't nod. He just stood there, looking into the trees. Fargo figured he wasn't used to dealing with dead bodies.

"Don't worry about those two," Fargo said. "They were going to kill you. Probably killed others before now."

"I guess," Dave said, still looking into the trees. "I'm not much of a gunhand. I mostly use my pistol to shoot snakes. Maybe once or twice a year. Rattlers. I don't bother the others."

"If those two had been born snakes, they'd have been rattlers. Somebody was going to pay them if they killed you. You got any idea who that somebody might be?"

Dave turned to Fargo, eyes wide with surprise. "Kill me? I don't even know anybody around these parts. Like I said, I was on my way to Hot Springs to look for my pa."

"What's he doing there?"

"I don't even know for sure if he's there," Dave said. "I just know that's where he was going."

"For the waters?"

"That's right. Me and Pa have a little farm up north of here. Got a few cattle, too. A couple of years ago, Pa fell out of the barn loft and hurt his leg. It got to painin' him something awful. A fella we knew told him the mineral waters in Hot Springs might do him some good, make the hurtin' stop."

That made sense to Fargo. The Quapaw Indians had believed in the healing powers of the springs for as far back as anybody could remember, and after Arkansas got to be a territory, the United States Congress had made the springs and surrounding mountains a federal reservation. Not too many Indians used the springs now, but a sizable settlement of whites had sprung up. People came from all over to bathe in the waters and get healed. And if they didn't get healed, they at least got warm. The springs were mighty hot.

"Pa's name's Steven," Dave went on. "That leg got to hurtin' him so bad that he figured the springs were worth a try. He's been gone from the farm for a long time now. Over a year. Ma and me, we never heard a word. That's not like Pa. Ma passed on a while back, and since she don't need me to take care of her, I thought I'd see if I could find Pa, let him know what happened."

"Looks like something was about to happen to you," Fargo said. "You reckon it has anything to do with your pa?"

Dave shook his head. "Didn't you hear what I just said?"

The Trailsman didn't take offense. "I heard you. I just wondered if your pa might have any enemies in Hot Springs."

"He didn't know anybody there. Me, neither."

Fargo thought about that. It didn't make a lot of sense for two men to be paid to kill Dave if nobody had any enemies.

Unless Brady and Paulie had thought Dave was somebody else. Like Skye Fargo.

But Fargo couldn't think of anybody who'd want to kill him. The only person he knew in Hot Springs was Angelique Leblanc, and she didn't have any reason to kill him. She was the one who'd asked him to come there. She hadn't said why, though. Fargo had been hoping she just wanted to see him and have a little fun, but maybe she was in some kind of trouble.

"Your pa have anybody looking for him?" Fargo said.

"He didn't hardly know anybody. I can't think of anyone who would be looking for him other than me."

"Well, we got to get these two dead fellas to town," Fargo said. "I'll gather up their guns. You see about the horses."

Dave nodded, looking glad for an excuse to get away from the bodies. He went off to round up the horses, and Fargo took a look at the bodies to see if there was anything that might let him know who wanted Dave dead.

There wasn't. Fargo found nothing much at all. Some tobacco and matches, a few coins, and that was it. He gathered up the pistols and the Henry, putting the pistols into his own saddlebags and giving the Henry to Dave, who'd come back with the horses.

"You might want to keep the rifle," Fargo said. "You never know when it might come in handy."

"I'm not much of a shot. Anyway, it don't seem right."

"They bushwhacked you and were trying to kill you, remember. And they tried even harder to kill me. It's not like we're stealing from them. They won't need it anymore."

"What about their horses and tack?"

"We'll see what we can get at the livery stable in Hot Springs and use it to bury them."

"I don't want the rifle," Dave said.

He was young, Fargo thought. He'd learn. Maybe. You never could tell.

"Whatever you say. Now let's see about giving these two fellas a ride."

Dave overcame his squeamishness well enough to help the Trailsman get the remains of Brady and Paulie up across their saddles and then tie them on their horses.

"You ready to get out of here?" Fargo said.

"Been ready since I got here," Dave told him.

2

Hot Springs was nestled down in a valley at the base of the green mountains, and it was a nice-sized town with hotels, bathhouses, and saloons. The springs around the town had steam rising off the water, and Fargo saw people splashing around in a couple of them. After a few weeks on the trail, he had to admit that a dip was mighty tempting, but it would have to wait.

Dave and Fargo got plenty of curious looks as they rode down the main street leading a pair of horses with dead bodies slung across them. A couple of little boys ran out into the street to get a closer look, and their mothers dashed out to snatch them back.

Fargo stopped to ask where the undertaker was, and a man pointed to a side street.

"Just down that way. Carpenter and coffin maker and undertaker all in one," the man said. "Marshal will want to know about those dead men."

"We'd like to talk to him," Fargo said. "Why don't you tell him where we are?"

"I'll do that," the man said, and he started off up the street.

Fargo and Dave found the undertaker without any trouble. He was set up in a barnlike building with an office in front. The sign on the building announced his skills and said that his name was Corby Carson. He stood out front working on some kind of cabinet when they rode up.

"We have some business for you," Fargo said.

Carson looked up from his cabinet. He was scrawny and undersized, older than Fargo had thought at first glance, probably well over sixty, with white hair and a wispy white beard.

"Looks like you do, at that," he said. "What happened? Snake bite 'em?"

Fargo grinned. "Yeah. Now they need burying."

"Well, get 'em inside here, and I'll see what I can do. You the one payin'?"

"After I see what their horses and tack will bring."

"Oughta be plenty to cover it." Carson turned and went inside the building through the wide front door.

Fargo followed, leading the horses. There was plenty of room. Dave hung back for a minute, looking all around. He'd been doing that ever since they got into town, but he didn't appear to have seen anybody he knew. After a few seconds, he followed Fargo into the building.

Carson led the way to the back, where the sun didn't reach. Fargo blinked to let his eyes adjust to the dim light.

"Just roll 'em onto these here boards," Carson said, indicating two pairs of sawhorses that supported thick pine boards about seven feet long.

"You get a lot of customers, do you?" Fargo said.

Corby shook his head. "Not that many. This is a quiet little place. I just like to be prepared."

"Good idea," Fargo said. He dismounted and untied the bodies. Dave came over and helped. He didn't even recoil when they had to drag Brady and Paulie off the horses and lay out their bodies. Maybe he was getting used to handling them.

14

"I'll get to work on a couple of coffins real soon now," Carson said. "Get the gravediggers lined up, too. What kind of send-off you want to give 'em? I can give a real nice service, even get a preacher if you want one."

"It's not like we knew these two," Fargo said. "Just get 'em in the ground."

"Well, I can do that, too. I guess you'll be wantin' the cheap coffins, then."

"Cheapest you can make."

"No flowers, either, I'll bet."

"You'd win," Fargo said.

"All right, then. And now you better get ready to tell what happened to these fellas, 'cause I think that's the town marshal comin' in the door up front."

Fargo turned and saw a big man silhouetted in the door. He had on a tall hat that made him seem even bigger. He walked to the back, and he didn't get any smaller along the way. Fargo was tall, but the marshal was taller. He'd have been taller even without the hat.

"Who are you fellas?" he said. His deep voice seemed to come from the bottom of a well. "What happened to these men?"

"Snake bit 'em," Carson said.

The marshal didn't smile. "I wasn't asking you, Corby, and you're not near as funny as you think you are." He nodded in Fargo's direction. "I was asking these two."

"The two men on the boards there ambushed us on our way into town," Fargo said. He thought he'd keep the story as simple as possible. He'd always found that was the best way. "Turned out we were better shots than they were."

The marshal didn't comment on the story. He said, "What're your names?"

"Name's Skye Fargo," the Trailsman said. "This is Dave Harragan."

15

"My name's Tatum, Hank Tatum," the marshal said.

Tatum didn't offer to shake hands, and neither did Fargo. Tatum stepped over to the sawhorses to get a better look at the bodies. "I know those two. Paulie Vinson and Brady Fennel. Been hanging around town for a while, gambling and drinking in the saloons. Been in a couple of fights. No-goods, if you ask me."

"I wouldn't argue with you," Fargo said.

"I guess they got what was coming to 'em," Tatum said. "No need to make a fuss over 'em."

"Wouldn't argue with that either."

"They been losing at the tables. Might've needed money."

"They said they were going to be paid for killing somebody," Fargo pointed out.

Tatum looked thoughtful, then dismissed the idea. "They might've meant they'd get paid with whatever they took from whoever they killed."

"Wouldn't have gotten much from me," Fargo said. He wasn't so sure the marshal was right about the payment.

Tatum looked him over. "Guess not. You ever go by any name besides Fargo?"

"Some call me the Trailsman."

"Thought so. I heard about you. One of those fellas trouble seems to follow around. Hope you didn't come here to cause any."

"Just came for the waters."

"Good." Tatum looked at Dave. "You say your name's Harragan?"

Dave hadn't spoken at all, and he still didn't. He just nodded.

"Any kin to Steve Harragan?" Tatum asked.

That got Dave's attention. He looked a bit puzzled. "Steve?"

"That's what I said. You know him?"

"Do you?"

"Ever'body around here knows him. You related?"

"He's my pa. Steven Harragan. I came here lookin' for him."

"Well, you found him. Almost. He's out of town on some kind of business, but he's due back tomorrow. I expect he'd want you to put up at his hotel. One of the best in town."

Dave looked excited at the prospect. "I never stayed in a hotel before. Which one is it?"

"Big one at the end of the main street. Right by one of the big springs. Good location. Stays full most of the time, but they'll have a room for you, bein' as how you're Steve's son. Better get on over there before it gets any later. Place fills up sometimes."

"What about Fargo?" Dave said.

"I guess he'd be welcome if he's a friend of yours."

"He's a friend, all right," Dave said.

"I am," Fargo said, "but I already have other accommodations."

"Where's that?" Tatum said.

"My business," Fargo said.

"Guess it is, at that, long as you don't cause any trouble." Tatum took off his big hat and brushed the crown, then settled it back on his head. "I'll leave you two alone to your business. Corby, you take care of those bodies right quick. Don't want 'em smellin' up the town."

"You know me, Marshal."

"Yeah, I do. That's why I told you to be quick about it."

Tatum looked at Fargo and Dave again, nodded, and left.

"Nice fella," Fargo said.

"Yeah," Carson said. "Right."

"You know my pa?" Dave said.

"Ever'body knows Steve Harragan, or knows of him. I don't know him more'n to say howdy to. We ain't exactly what you'd call buddies."

"He wear an eye patch?"

"Matter of fact, he does. Don't know why."

"That's him," Dave said. "That's my pa. He got in a fight when he was a boy and lost an eye." He paused. "I wonder why he never wrote me and Ma, what with him bein' such a big shot here. I wonder how he wound up in the money."

Carson turned away. "Gotta get to work. Gotta get these fellas in the ground right quick. Don't have any more time to talk."

He pulled a tape measure out from somewhere and walked over to some boards that leaned against the wall. Ignoring Dave and Fargo, he started to measure the boards.

"Time for us to split up," Fargo told Dave. "I'll see about getting these horses sold, and you can get settled at your pa's hotel."

Dave didn't argue. He stuck out his hand.

"Been mighty nice meetin' you, Mr. Fargo, and thanks for all you did. I wouldn't be here if it wasn't for you."

"Glad to help out," the Trailsman said, shaking Dave's hand. "You watch yourself around here. You still don't know why those two wanted to kill you."

"Some kinda mistake," Dave said. "Had to be, or it was like the marshal said and they were just planning on robbing me."

"Maybe," Fargo said. "You watch out, anyway. You sure you don't want the Henry?"

"Wouldn't do me any good. Got no use for a gun like that. You can sell it, maybe."

"I'll do that," Fargo said. "You take care now."

"I will," Dave said.

Fargo watched the young man leave and wondered if he really would take care, or if he even knew how.

Fargo got a good price for the horses and tack, and then went to the little hardware store in town to sell the rifle and pistols. He got a fair deal, and he promised himself that he'd get the money to the kid as soon as he could. Dave would try to turn it down, but Fargo thought he could convince him to take it without too much persuasion.

After he'd arranged for the Ovaro's keep, Fargo left the livery stable and walked around town for a few minutes to look the place over. Harragan's hotel, the Grand, was by far the finest of the ones in town, though one nearby, the Superior, looked almost as fine. Fargo wasn't interested in finery, however. He was interested in Angelique Leblanc. So he went looking for her.

Fargo had met Angelique in Saint Louis a few years earlier. She had been a saloon girl with ambitions, and she was smarter than most. She understood the value of money and its uses, and unlike most women in her profession, she was saving hers.

Saint Louis was the starting point for a lot of wagon trains, and Fargo was there to lead one of them on its journey. He'd heard a ruckus one night after leaving a saloon and had rescued Angelique from three men who'd had too much to drink and decided to get some free services from Angelique in the alley.

After he'd taken care of the men, Angelique had thanked him with the kind of treatment the men had been denied. The Trailsman liked her, and she liked him, too. They'd met a couple of other times before he left, and she'd told him that she didn't plan to stay where she was, that one day she'd have a place of her own.

And now she did. She'd opened a saloon called the

Arkansas Traveler in Hot Springs, and she'd sent word to Fargo inviting him for a visit. He thought there might be more to it than a simple invitation, however. He and Angelique had enjoyed their short time together, as Fargo had enjoyed himself with other women, but it had meant little more than that to either of them. However, just before Fargo had left with the wagons, he'd told her that if she ever needed him to let him know. He wondered if she needed him now.

He found the saloon easily enough. It was several blocks from the Grand Hotel, not near enough to any of the springs to get any bathers to stop in for a casual visit on their way to the waters, but then Fargo didn't think Angelique was interested in that kind of business. She'd want the people who planned to stay a while and enjoy everything the saloon had to offer.

A big sign hung over the entrance to the saloon. Over the words The Arkansas Traveler, there was a picture of a man on a horse. The man was looking at another man who sat on the porch of a ramshackle house. The man was playing a fiddle, and a sleeping dog lay at his feet.

Fargo knew the story of the Arkansas Traveler, and he could even hum a little of the tune if he was of a mind to. But he was seldom of a mind to do that sort of thing.

As he admired the picture, the Trailsman heard rising voices inside the saloon. He pushed through the saloon's batwing doors and went into the dim light of the interior, giving the place a quick once-over.

To his left was a long, polished bar with a mirror behind it. A skinny bartender stood in back of the bar, looking at two men who had their backs to Fargo. They were arguing with a tall, beautiful brunette— Angelique Leblanc herself. Other men sat around at tables, some of them with drinks, some of them with cards in their hands. A couple of saloon girls stood off to one side, near a beat-up upright piano. A man sat at the piano, but he wasn't playing a tune. Like everyone else in the place, he was looking at Angelique and the two men.

Fargo looked around for the bouncer, but he didn't see one. He wondered where the man could be. Angelique was too smart to try to run a saloon without a bouncer.

No one had noticed Fargo come in, not even Angelique. He started across the floor, avoiding the tables in his path, and her eyes widened when she saw him.

The two men who were arguing with her must have noticed something because they turned toward Fargo. Fargo ignored the angry glance they shot in his direction.

"Angelique," Fargo said. "It's a pleasure to see you again."

"Who the hell are you?" the man on Fargo's left said. He had a bristly beard, and his eyes were red, as if he'd been drinking too much.

"Yeah," the other man said. He was short and thick around the middle, built like a barrel. "Who the hell are you?"

"Must be an echo in here," Fargo said.

The two men looked at each other.

"A smart-ass," the bearded one said.

"Asshole," the round one responded.

The two men laughed, and the bearded man took a couple of steps forward until he was standing a foot or so from Fargo. He poked the Trailsman in the chest with his index finger.

"I asked you who the hell you were," he said.

Fargo stood his ground. "Name's Fargo. What's yours?"

"None of your damn business. Why don't you just have yourself a drink and leave us be?"

Fargo pushed the man's hand aside and looked past

him. "Are these two fellas friends of yours, Angelique? Or would you like for me to throw them out of here?"

"It's all right, Skye," Angelique said. "We were just having a discussion."

"It ain't all right," the bearded man said. "You heard me, Fargo. Move on."

Fargo shook his head. "I don't think so."

"Then we'll have to move you," the short man said.

"You can try."

The bearded man laughed and swung at Fargo, bringing his fist upward from below his waist. If the blow had landed, it would have crushed a couple of Fargo's prized possessions, but the Trailsman made a half turn, grabbed the man's arm, and slung him hard into his barrel-shaped companion.

The two men collided and had to grab hold of each other to stay upright as they did an awkward dance toward the bar. They banged into a table and almost fell over a chair.

"They make a handsome couple, don't they?" Fargo said. "Not much good at waltzing, though."

The men didn't think Fargo was funny. As soon as they'd gotten their balance, they both charged at him.

The short one lowered his head in an attempt to butt the Trailsman. Fargo stepped aside at the last second and hammered the top of his head with the edge of his fist. The man kept going for a couple of stumbling steps before hitting the floor on his face and skidding ahead for a few feet. He came to a stop with his head against the leg of one of the card tables.

Fargo didn't have time to enjoy the sight because the bearded man swung a ham-sized fist at him, much higher than the last time. Fargo ducked under the whistling blow. He slipped past the man and slammed him twice in the kidneys. The man went to his knees, and Fargo kicked him in the back of the head, sending him sliding along the floor in the general direction of his friend.

The two men lay there for a few seconds before they rolled over and started to go for their guns.

Fargo said, "Just sit there for a minute and think things over."

They blinked and looked in his direction. Fargo had his .44 in his right hand, and it was pointed straight at them.

"I'd hate to have to shoot you and get blood all over Miss Angelique's floor," Fargo said. "She wouldn't like that."

"No," Angelique said. "I wouldn't."

"But I'll do it anyway if they make me," Fargo said.

The men didn't say anything. They kept their hands well away from their pistols as they got to their feet.

"I think it's time for you to leave," Fargo said.

They glared at him, but they left. Fargo had thought they might tell him how sorry he'd be for roughing them up, but they kept silent.

Fargo watched them until they'd gone through the batwings and out into the sunlight. Fargo holstered the .44. Angelique stood beside him.

"Thanks, Skye," she said.

"My pleasure. Who were those two?"

Angelique looked around the saloon. Now that the fun was over, things were back to normal and the few customers resumed their activities. The cardplayers bid their hands, the drinkers downed their liquor, the women draped themselves over prospective customers. The piano man started up a tune. "The Arkansas Traveler," of course.

"Let's have a drink and talk about it somewhere else," Angelique said. She took the Trailsman's arm. "It's good to see you, Skye."

Fargo looked down into her bright blue eyes. "It's good to see you, too."

Angelique gave a signal to the bartender with her free hand and pulled Fargo with her toward the stairs leading to the building's second floor where Angelique had her private room with a canopy bed, rugs on the floor, and an overstuffed chair with doilies on the headrest and arms. The washstand beside the dresser held a pitcher and bowl with intricate flowered patterns on them. The same flowered pattern adorned a tall modesty screen. The room seemed mighty fancy to Fargo, though Fargo didn't think Angelique needed the screen.

"You must be doing well," he said.

"Well enough."

Angelique went to the door and took a bottle of whiskey and two glasses that the barman handed her.

"Thanks, Albert," she said. He nodded and left.

Angelique held up the bottle for Fargo to admire. "The good stuff. Have a seat, Skye."

Fargo avoided the overstuffed chair and sat in a sturdy wooden one nearby. Angelique handed him the whiskey and set the glasses on the table before seating herself in the big chair. She poured them both a generous splash of whiskey.

Fargo waited until he'd had a sip of the fiery liquid to say, "You want to tell me what that was all about?"

Angelique looked at him over the rim of her glass. "I'd like to think it was just two toughs making trouble for the hell of it."

"But that's not what you really think," Fargo said.

"No, it's not. I think it has something to do with a lot of other things."

"You want to tell me about the other things?"

Angelique leaned back in the chair. "You'll think I didn't want to see you again."

"I know you wanted to see me. I thought there might be a little more to it than that, though."

"There is." Angelique sipped her whiskey. "Something's going on, but I'm not sure what. George Lindsey left the other day. George was my bouncer."

"When you say he left, what does that mean?"

"It means he didn't show up for work. Didn't say good-bye, didn't draw his pay. Since then, there've been a few incidents like the one you walked in on, rowdies causing a ruckus, stirring up trouble. Albert's not much help. He's a good barman, but he's not a fighter. He keeps a shotgun under the bar, but he's never used it. I'm not sure he ever would."

"You think there's a reason for all the trouble?" Fargo said.

"I do," Angelique said. "You want more whiskey?"

Fargo set his glass on the table between them. "Don't mind if I do."

As she refilled both their glasses, Fargo admired the womanly curves that were hardly hidden by her clothing. He wasn't surprised that she needed help of some kind, but he hoped that her problems, whatever they were, wouldn't stand in the way of other kinds of activities.

"I think Steve Harragan wants to buy the saloon," Angelique said. "But I don't want to sell it."

"Harragan," Fargo said. "He's a big man in Hot Springs, I hear."

"The biggest. He's got money, and he likes to spend it. When he sees something he wants, he goes after it."

Fargo thought about that. It didn't fit with what he'd been told about Harragan by Dave.

"So Harragan is sending people here to cause trouble," Fargo mused. "They bother the customers enough, you'll lose business. You lose business, you lose money.

25

When you've lost enough, Harragan can persuade you that you might as well sell him the saloon."

"That's what I think. I can't prove it. Doesn't matter who it is that's causing the problems. I'm not going to be run out."

"How about the marshal?" Fargo asked. "Tatum. Can't he put a stop to the trouble?"

Angelique shook her head, and black curls tumbled about her face. "He's not much help. I've sent for him a time or two, but by the time he arrives, the trouble is over."

"This Harragan," Fargo said. "You sure the saloon's all he wants?"

Angelique smiled. "Well, there might be something else. He can't have that, either."

"What are my chances?"

"We'll see. Do you think you can help me?"

"That depends," Fargo said.

"On what?"

"I'm not sure," Fargo said. "We'll have to find out. Isn't it about time for supper?"

"Close enough. We don't serve food here, though."

"How about the Grand Hotel?"

"Yes, there's a dining room there."

"You think Albert can handle things while we're gone?"

"I don't think there'll be any more trouble until later, when we're back. I hope not."

Fargo hoped not, too.

"Then why don't you and I see what they have to eat?" he said.

3

Fargo felt a little out of place in his buckskins when they entered the hotel dining room. It was lit by a huge chandelier festooned with coal-oil lamps, and the elegant furnishings looked more like a picture in a book than the kind of thing you'd expect to find in Arkansas.

It was a good thing he was with Angelique because nobody noticed Fargo. Angelique was by far the most beautiful woman in the place, and all the men looked at her. So did all the women, though not for the same reasons.

A waiter in fancy clothes walked them to a table. When they were seated, Fargo said, "You ever been here before?"

"Just once. With Harragan, when he tried to talk me into selling to him."

"Is that all he tried to talk you into?"

"What do you think?"

Fargo smiled. Before he could answer, Dave Harragan walked into the room. Fargo was expecting him. He'd stopped at the desk and sent a message to Dave, asking the young man to join them. Fargo motioned him over before the waiter could seat him.

Dave was a bit shy on seeing Fargo's dinner companion, and his face reddened when Fargo introduced her. Fargo covered the awkwardness by passing Dave his share of the money from the horses and guns.

"I can't take this," Dave said when Fargo told him what it was.

"Sure you can. You earned it by nearly getting killed. You might as well get the benefit of it."

"Don't seem right, somehow. You're the one who saved my ass."

As soon as he'd said the last word, Dave blushed a deep red. "Sorry about that, Miz Leblanc. I didn't mean to offend."

Angelique smiled. "Believe me, Mr. Harragan, I've heard worse."

"I can't hardly believe that, ma'am."

"Call me Angelique."

Fargo had explained Dave's situation to her as they walked to the hotel. She couldn't figure things any better than he could, though she said that later she'd tell him the story about Harragan showing up in Hot Springs.

"You keep this money," Fargo said, pressing it on Dave. "You'll need it while you're here if your pa doesn't come back soon."

"Oh, he'll be here tomorrow," Dave said. "That's what they told me at the desk. Said they'd heard I might be showing up, and they'd saved a room for me."

"How'd they know you'd be here?" Fargo said.

"They didn't say. I guess my pa's been gettin' my letters right along, even if he didn't answer 'em. He must've told the folks who work here."

"That's probably it," Fargo said.

The waiter brought menus. After seeing the prices, Dave said he was glad he'd taken the money.

"Your pa's not footing the food bill?" Fargo said.

"Not that I know of."

"Well, save your money. I'll cover it this time. You can treat me the next."

Dave didn't want to accept, but Angelique told him it was the right thing to do, and he relented. He asked if Angelique lived in Hot Springs.

"I own a saloon," she said. "The Arkansas Traveler. Come in for a drink. It's on the house."

Dave nodded, thanked her, and blushed again. Fargo figured he didn't get off the farm much. Getting away for a while was going to be an education for the kid.

"Do you know my pa?" Dave asked Angelique when he'd recovered his composure.

"We've met," Angelique said. "On a matter of business."

"My pa must be pretty big in business," Dave said. He looked around the room. "I'd never have thought he could have anything like this. He had enough trouble just keeping up with the business of the farm."

A waiter came and took their orders. When he'd left, Dave said, "Pa never even let Ma and me know he'd hit it big. I just can't make any sense of it. I know he loved Ma, and you'd think he'd have wanted me and her to have a little part in this."

"Sometimes men do strange things," Angelique said. "Believe me, I know."

Dave didn't blush, but he looked down at the floor.

"I don't mean he took up with a woman here," Angelique said. "He didn't. You shouldn't think that."

"If you say so. This whole thing is hard for me to get used to. I thought maybe my pa was dead or that his leg had got so bad he couldn't get back, but to hear that he's rich and owns a big hotel, well, it's not easy to take in."

"He can clear it all up for you when he comes back tomorrow," Angelique said. "I'm sure there's a good reason for everything."

Their meals arrived, steak for Fargo and Dave, fried chicken for Angelique. The food was good, and they didn't do much talking until they were finished.

"I'd like to meet your pa," Fargo said, wiping his lips with a big napkin and laying it on the table. "After the two of you hash things out, I mean."

"I'd like you to meet him," Dave said. "He'd be happy to shake the hand of the man who saved my life. You come around tomorrow or the next day. I'd be proud to introduce you."

Fargo agreed, and Dave thanked him for the meal before going up to his room. After Fargo paid the bill, he and Angelique walked back to the saloon. The dark autumn sky was speckled with stars, and the moon was near full. A little chill hung in the air. Fargo slipped his arm around Angelique's waist.

"There's something I want to ask you, Skye," she said.

"What might that be?"

"How'd you like a job?"

That wasn't what Fargo had expected to hear. "A job? What kind of job?"

"I'm afraid the trouble at my place is going to get worse. I need a bouncer. When I sent word that I'd like to see you, I meant it, but I have to admit I thought you might be able to help me, too."

"I wasn't looking for a job," Fargo said.

"It's not just a job. There'd be other . . . benefits."

Fargo smiled. "What would those be?"

"There'd be the pay, of course, and you'd have a place to stay. You could enjoy the springs. You'd have companionship."

"Companionship," Fargo said. "Now that's a right nice word."

Angelique snuggled herself against him. "You know what I mean."

"I think I do, at that," Fargo said, "but you don't have to make the offer or even pay me. I'm glad to help out a friend."

"I thought you would be, but the workman is worthy of his hire."

"I didn't know you could quote the Bible."

"I've heard it said that even the Devil can quote scripture."

"And I can even recognize a little Shakespeare now and then," Fargo said.

"I guess we both do a little reading."

"Don't have much time for it now. Maybe I will while I'm visiting you."

They had reached the saloon, and Angelique moved away from Fargo a little.

"It would be nice to think so," she said. "But I have my doubts."

Fargo did, too. They went up the step onto the boardwalk and entered the saloon. The piano man played "Oh! Susanna." Fargo looked around. He didn't count the people at the tables and the bar, but he could have done so easily enough.

"Business always like this?" he said.

Angelique frowned. "It is now. It wasn't like this before the trouble started. I'd have twice as many people here, maybe three times as many."

Fargo walked over to the bar. Albert polished an already sparkling glass and looked at the two customers who stood at the far end of the bar. The two men didn't look back.

"Any trouble tonight, Albert?" Fargo said.

"Not so far." Albert looked at the two men again.

"You recognize those two?" Fargo said.

The men didn't look like people who'd visit Hot Springs for the baths. In fact, their clothing was sweat-stained and dirty, and they didn't appear to have had a bath of any kind recently.

"I think they've been in before." Albert lowered his voice. "If you know what I mean."

"I think I do. Here's something you don't know, though. Miss Leblanc has hired me to look out for the place, handle any trouble that comes up. You don't mind, do you?"

Albert bent down and set the glass on a shelf under the bar. "What did you say your name was?"

"I didn't say, but it's Skye Fargo."

Albert put the towel on the bar and extended his hand. "I'm glad to meet you, Mr. Fargo. Mighty glad."

They shook hands, and Fargo went to join Angelique, who stood by the piano, talking to one of the saloon girls.

"Things seem pretty quiet," Fargo said.

"So far," Angelique said. "Skye, this is Rose."

Rose was a buxom blonde who didn't mind displaying her assets in a low-cut dress. She smiled a professional smile and told Fargo she was happy to make his acquaintance.

"The piano player's Sam Hawkins," Angelique said.

"Pleased to meet you," Hawkins said. He was a thin man with big hands and lean fingers. A toothpick dangled from his lips and bobbed a little as he spoke. "Angelique says you're going to handle any trouble that comes along."

Fargo nodded.

"Then you'd better watch out for those two at the bar," Hawkins said. "They've been quiet so far, but they raised Cain the last time they were here."

"Albert told me," Fargo said. "Could be they just want a drink."

"Could be," Hawkins said. "Be nice if that were all."

Hawkins' tone indicated he didn't think the men were there just to have a quiet drink.

"We'll see," Fargo said.

"Why don't we go upstairs," Angelique said to him. "I'll show you your room."

Fargo nodded to Hawkins and Rose, who gave him a lascivious grin, and followed Angelique up the stairs. She got a lamp from her own room and led him to the last room on the hall and opened the door.

"I'm afraid it's not quite as nice as my room," she said, entering and holding up the lamp.

In the flickering light, Fargo saw a bed, a chair, and a washstand. The floor was bare, but Fargo didn't mind. It was clean, and the bedclothes looked clean as well. He'd spent more nights than one in a lot worse places.

"It'll do me just fine," he said.

He was about to ask Angelique if she had any interest in testing the mattress when he heard someone shout from downstairs. The shout was followed by more noises.

"Looks like my job just started," Fargo said. "You stay here. I'll see what's going on."

Fargo strode to the head of the stairs. Angelique was right behind him.

"I thought I told you to stay in the room," Fargo said, turning to her.

Angelique gave him a look. "This is my saloon. I'm the boss here."

Fargo grinned. "I guess I forgot."

He looked down at the saloon floor. The two men from the bar now stood at the piano. One of them was holding Hawkins by both arms while the other sat on the piano stool. An overturned table lay nearby. As Fargo watched, the man started to play. He wasn't very good, and Fargo had no idea what the tune was supposed to be.

The man started to sing. He had a high, light voice,

and most of the words were slurred. The tune he was singing didn't quite match the one he was playing. Or trying to play. Fargo wondered how many drinks Albert had served him.

"That should get rid of all the music lovers," Fargo told Angelique. "I'll go down and see if I can quiet that fella down."

He went down the stairs and saw that the customers had diminished considerably in number since the new piano player had taken over.

When the Trailsman reached the bottom of the stairs, he had to yell to make himself heard over the raucous singing and the pitiful piano pounding.

"That's about enough music," he said. "If that's what you call it. I've enjoyed all I can stand."

The man who held Hawkins put his foot in Hawkins' back and shoved him into Fargo as hard as he could. Hawkins grabbed at Fargo in an attempt to keep upright, and Fargo was reminded of the odd little dance the two men had done earlier that day.

As Fargo tried to disentangle himself from Hawkins, he saw the piano player kick back the stool, stand up, and turn around. He and the other man both reached for their guns, and Fargo realized that neither of them was drunk. They'd set him up, and he'd walked right into it.

Now they were going to try to kill him.

Fargo pushed Hawkins aside as the two men drew their pistols.

The remaining customers scattered. Some of them ducked under tables, and a couple jumped over the bar and disappeared behind it, joining Albert who was already there.

Hawkins hit the floor and rolled over.

Fargo palmed out his .44 as a bullet buzzed past his

right ear. Glass shattered behind him, but he didn't look to see what had happened. A second bullet took off his hat as he triggered a shot of his own.

A crimson stain bloomed on the chest of the man who'd played the piano, or tried to, and he fell backward onto the instrument, making a discordant noise as he hit the keys. It sounded little worse than his attempt at playing. His blood stained the ivory keys.

The second man fired again, and Fargo felt the bullet tug at the left arm of his buckskins. He pulled the trigger of the .44 twice, and the man dropped his pistol. His fingers went to his throat, but they couldn't stop the blood that pumped out. He toppled over and fell across the man who was already on the floor.

The big room was filled with the acrid smell of gun smoke, and Fargo's ears rang from the sound of the shots. The two men on the floor lay still except a twitch of one hand. Fargo looked around to see if they'd brought anyone else with them. No one made a move on Fargo, and he relaxed a little.

Hawkins pushed himself to a seated position by one end of the piano, and Rose bent down to see if he was all right. Angelique came to stand beside Fargo.

"Are you all right?" she asked.

"Sure," Fargo told her. He looked at the two men again. "But they aren't."

"Dead?"

"Should be. I didn't have time to be careful with them. You know who they are?"

"No. They've been here before, but all they did was push some customers around and bother the girls. I never thought they'd do something like this."

"Looks like I'm going to earn my pay, all right," Fargo said.

"You already have," Angelique said.

She might have said more, but just then Marshal Tatum shoved through the batwings. His tall hat brushed the lintel.

"What the hell's going on here?" he said. He saw Fargo, and he saw the dead men. "Jesus wept, Fargo. Did you kill those two?"

"Sure did," Fargo said. "Seemed like the thing to do at the time."

Tatum sounded disgusted. He probably was. "You haven't been in town a whole day, and already you killed four men. And I told you I didn't want any trouble."

Fargo started to tell Tatum that he hadn't killed four men in town, but only two. However, he didn't think that argument would carry any weight with Tatum at the moment. Maybe when the marshal calmed down a little, he'd see it that way. Or maybe it wouldn't matter to him.

"It wasn't Fargo who caused the trouble," Angelique said. She nodded toward the bodies. "It was them. You can ask anybody who was here."

Fargo noticed that there was hardly anybody left in the saloon. Most of those who hadn't left earlier had gotten out as soon as the marshal arrived.

"She's right, Marshal," Hawkins said. He still sat on the floor. "They roughed me up and tried to kill Fargo."

Tatum raised a hand as if to brush the comment away. "I'd expect you to say that. You work here."

"It's the truth," a man said. One of the gamblers. He didn't appear too shaken by the events. "I'd be willing to testify to that."

"So would I," Alfred called, rising up from behind the bar. He had wet stains on his shirt from a bottle broken by one of the bullets.

"Me, too," Rose said, and the other saloon girls nodded.

36

"All right, damn it," Tatum said. "I won't arrest you, Fargo, but I'd sure as hell like to. Who were those men?"

"Never saw them before," Fargo said. "I hear they've caused trouble in here other times, though."

"There's been too damn much trouble in here lately," Tatum said. "But by God, there better not be any more. Especially not like this. If there is, I'll close this damn place down so fast it'll make your head swim."

"You don't have to worry," Angelique said. "We won't have any more trouble." She looked at the Trailsman. "Fargo's hired on as the bouncer."

Tatum wasn't mollified. "Damn it, that sounds like trouble right there. The man's a killer."

Fargo didn't like what the marshal said one bit, but he wasn't going to make an issue of it and antagonize Tatum any further. He said, "I'm not going to start any trouble, Marshal, but if somebody else starts something, I might have to finish it."

"You sure finished those poor sonsabitches," Tatum said.

He might have said more, but the batwing doors swung open and Corby Carson bustled in, rubbing his hands together, whether from the chill outside or in anticipation of more business, it was hard to tell.

"I hear you got some more customers for me," he said, and then he saw the two bodies. "Yep, there they are." He eyed the bodies. "I'm bettin' it's gonna be two more of the cheap boxes."

"You'll have to ask Miz Leblanc," Tatum said. "It's up to her. I know for damn sure the county's not paying you to plant 'em."

"How about it?" Corby said, grinning at Angelique. "You want to give 'em a fine send-off?"

"You know better, Corby," Angelique said. "I'll pay, but only for the cheapest job you can do."

"Sure is hard for a fella to make an honest livin' off the dyin' around here," Corby said, shaking his head. He chuckled. "But I gotta admit that things have picked up right smart since you got to town, Fargo."

That didn't make Tatum any happier. "That's the damn truth, but it better stop right now."

"I promise I won't shoot anybody who doesn't shoot at me first," Fargo said. "Corby, you got any idea who those two were?"

Carson walked over to the bodies and looked down at them. One man's arm was draped over the other's face. Carson toed the arm and moved it aside.

"Nope, don't know 'em. Seen 'em around town, maybe."

"How about you, Marshal?"

"Drifters," Tatum said, dismissing the dead men as he'd dismissed the earlier two. "Stopped here because of the springs. Get rid of 'em."

With that, he turned and left.

"Well, Fargo?" Corby said.

"Well, what?"

"Well, you gonna help me get these two fellas out of here and into my wagon? I can't do it myself, and you're the one who killed 'em."

"I'll help," Fargo said.

"Come on, then." Corby bent down and took the feet of the top man. "You get his shoulders."

Fargo slipped his hands into the man's armpits and lifted.

"Here we go," Corby said. "Clear the way. We're comin' through."

He didn't need to say it. Hardly anyone was left in the saloon, and everyone who was there ignored the men as they lugged the body outside.

4

The saloon didn't close until the last customer had gone home, but Fargo and Angelique went upstairs to her room around midnight. Fargo didn't think it would be worthwhile to anyone to start trouble now, not with only a couple of people still downstairs.

He and Angelique sat in the same chairs they'd taken earlier, and Angelique poured whiskey for both of them. They sipped in silence for a while, and then Angelique said, "What do you think, Skye?"

Fargo looked her over, admiring the strong line of her chin, the way her hair fell about her face, the shape of her body under her clothing.

"Think about what?" he said.

Angelique laughed. "I know what you're thinking, all right, but I didn't mean *that*. I meant what do you think about those two men you had to kill, about what's going on here."

"I don't know what to think," the Trailsman said, and he honestly didn't. "I just know those two men I shot were trying to kill me, and I know it was something they'd planned before they got here. You remember what I told you about Dave Harragan?"

"The two men who tried to kill him?"

"Yeah. What if it wasn't him they were after? What if they thought he was me? We were both riding in the same direction, both of us headed to Hot Springs."

"Why would anybody want to kill you?"

"That's what I'd like to know." Fargo paused. He didn't know how to say what he had to say next without making Angelique angry, but it had to be said. "Not too many people knew I was coming here."

Angelique looked down at the last of the amber liquid in her glass, then looked back up at Fargo. "I didn't tell anybody. The only one who knew you were coming was Seth Lansford, and that's because he was the one who took my message."

Fargo hadn't heard the message from Lansford but from a man named Tolson, who'd passed it on from Lansford.

"I guess more than one person got told along the way," Fargo said. "Others could've found out. I know you wouldn't have any reason to get rid of me. There's plenty who would, though, for one reason or another."

"Maybe one of them heard where you were headed," Angelique said. She put her glass on the table. "But not from me."

Fargo hadn't really thought so, but it was good to hear her say it. That didn't mean it was the truth, however. It was something he'd have to keep in the back of his mind while he considered some of the other possibilities. Over the years he'd made a lot of friends, but he'd also made more than his share of enemies.

"I knew you weren't trying to get rid of me," Fargo said. "You hired me, after all."

"That's right, and after what happened tonight, you can see why."

"You think Harragan's behind the trouble?"

"He wants to buy the saloon," Angelique said. "He

40

wants me. He can't have either one. What do you think?"

"Likely he's the root of the problem," Fargo agreed. "Except that he's not even in town."

"He could still be behind things. He was here when it started, and he'll be back soon."

"Tomorrow, the marshal said. You know anything about Tatum?"

"He keeps the peace," Angelique said. "Mostly."

"How about when you have trouble here?"

"He's not so good about it then, but he doesn't let things get out of hand."

Fargo wondered if Tatum and Harragan might be working together, or if Tatum was being paid off to let things slide if they happened at Angelique's place. Fargo had met a lot of lawmen in his travels, and while most of them were honest, there'd been a few who leaned the other way. But Fargo had never run into either Harragan or Tatum before, so if someone was trying to kill him, or have him killed, it likely wasn't one of those two.

"You know that other thing I was thinking about?" Fargo said.

Angelique smiled. "Of course."

"Why don't we do something about that?"

"Why not?" Angelique said.

Angelique stood up and put out her hand. Fargo took it and let her raise him from his chair.

"Come with me," Angelique said.

Fargo thought they were already right where they should be, or almost. It was only a few feet to the big canopy bed. He said, "Where are we going?"

"To the springs. It'll do us both good."

Fargo wasn't so sure, but after Angelique stopped at the washstand for a couple of towels, he let her lead him from the room.

When they descended the stairs, they saw Albert behind the bar, putting away the last of the glasses. One man was left at a table, but he was asleep, his head down on his arm. Hawkins the piano player was gone, and so were all the saloon girls. Most of the latter had rooms on the same floor where Fargo would stay, though a couple of them lived in town and used the rooms only when it was necessary for their jobs.

Angelique told Alfred to wake up the sleeper, send him away, and close up. Then she led Fargo through the deserted streets toward Harragan's hotel.

"Harragan bought the hotel not long after he got to town," Angelique said. "A man named Cole built it, and he was doing just fine. It's located by the best spring in the area, and he had plenty of business."

"Why'd he sell?" Fargo said, but he thought he had a pretty good idea already.

"Nobody knows," Angelique said. "There were rumors, but that's all."

"What kind of rumors?"

"That Cole was getting threats. There was trouble at the hotel, too."

"The same kind you're having?"

"Pretty much. Guests getting into fights that they claimed they never started, rowdies coming in and insulting the women, that kind of thing."

It seemed to Fargo like things were following a pattern. From what Angelique said, Harragan sounded like the kind of man who got what he wanted, one way or the other. If he couldn't persuade you to let him have it, he'd find some other means of getting it.

That didn't fit at all with what Dave had told Fargo, but that didn't mean it couldn't happen. It was possible that the man had been waiting for years for the chance to ditch his family and start a new life for himself without them. He might have faked his leg injury. He might even have been taking money from the farm and putting it aside for his own use. Fargo believed that people, most of them, were decent at their cores, but some of them were just downright sneaky and rotten, and there was no changing them.

They reached the hotel but didn't go inside. Angelique led Fargo on past it, around to the farther side where the pool was located. No one else was around. Steam rose above the water in the cool night air. Fargo smelled the scent of the pine trees that towered nearby. A small bathhouse stood on one side of the pool, but they didn't go inside that, either.

Angelique went to the edge of the pool and started to remove her clothes. Fargo wasn't exactly shy, but he wasn't sure that getting naked right next to the hotel was a good idea.

"Do you think anybody'll come by?" he said.

"I've done this before," Angelique said, not pausing in the removal of her dress or explaining when or why she'd done it. "Nobody's ever out at this time of night. You don't have to worry about your modesty."

Fargo decided to believe her. He stripped off his buckskin shirt. The night air prickled his skin, and he kicked off his boots. Glancing over at Angelique he caught a moonlit glimpse of white skin and a dark triangle of hair at the juncture of her thighs before she slid into the pool. Fargo unbuckled his gun belt, coiled it, and set it on his shirt. Then he slipped out of his trousers and joined her.

The water shocked him with its heat. It was hotter than he'd expected, and the contrast with the cool air made it seem even hotter. Fargo didn't know if it would cure anything, but it sure did give a fella something to think about.

"Doesn't it feel wonderful?" Angelique said.

Fargo wasn't sure how to answer. He didn't want to hurt her feelings, but he was pretty sure his private parts were going to be too blistered to do him any good later on. It was all he could do to keep his body under the water.

"Cat got your tongue?" Angelique said.

"It's mighty warm here," Fargo said. "I think maybe I'm boiling like a potato."

Angelique laughed. It was a good sound to hear, and Fargo hoped he was the only one who heard it. He'd hate for someone in the hotel to come out and investigate, or worse that someone who had it in for him would catch him there. It wasn't so much that he minded being seen without his clothes. The thing that bothered him was that a naked man was at a big disadvantage in a fight.

"You're not going to boil," Angelique said. "Just sit still for a little while and see."

Fargo did as she suggested, leaning back against the bank of the pool and letting the heat soak into him. Before long, he felt some of the day's tension disappearing from his body, almost as if the water were drawing it out. He looked up at the stars sprinkled across the dark sky, then closed his eyes. Before he knew it, he was almost asleep.

Angelique poked him in the ribs with her finger.

"Come over here," she said.

She wasn't far away, and Fargo slid over to join her. She pressed herself against him. He felt her soft breasts and the stiffness of her jutting nipples.

Her nipples weren't the only things that were stiff. It turned out that at least one part of Fargo hadn't been relaxed by the heated waters at all, and when Angelique slipped her hand down and gripped his erect pole, she knew it, too.

"My goodness," she said. "Is there a big snake loose in here?"

"Not a very dangerous one," Fargo said, his hand seeking the cleft mound between her legs. He found it and stroked the wet hair. After a second or two, he let his fingers slide downward, and Angelique opened her legs to accommodate them.

She looked up at Fargo, and he bent to kiss her. Their tongues did battle, and their kiss was as steamy as the water they sat in. Angelique began to stroke Fargo's rod, and he let a finger move slowly along the hairy slit between her legs.

Before long Angelique's hand was moving faster, and so was Fargo's finger. They broke their kiss, and Fargo began to suck Angelique's right breast, his tongue working on the nipple. Angelique threw back her head in delight.

After a moment, she put a hand on Fargo's chest and pushed him gently away. He started to protest, but she floated around in front of him, still keeping her grip on his tool. In spite of the buoyancy of her breasts, she was able to lower herself down onto him. Her smile when she was settled let him know how good she felt.

Fargo felt mighty fine himself. Angelique's breasts floated in front of him, the nipples grazing his chest as she straddled him and wiggled her hips. The warmth of the water was nothing compared to the warmth of the sweet honey pot that held Fargo within its grip.

Angelique rocked forward and back, then side to side, causing little tremors of pleasure in Fargo. He put his hands on her breasts and massaged the stiffened nipples.

"Harder," Angelique said, and when Fargo obliged, she bounced lightly up and down in the water, each time going just a little bit higher and sinking down a little harder on him, taking him as far inside as she could.

Soon she was bouncing so fast that she sent ripples rushing away from the two of them, ripples that swiftly crossed the pool and washed the opposite bank.

"Help me, Skye," she said. "Give it to me now."

Fargo gave it to her, bouncing along with her. The ripples increased in speed and size, and Fargo found the almost weightless feeling given by the support of the water, along with the heat and the relaxation, had increased his desire as well as Angelique's. She mashed her breasts against him as if trying to force the stony nipples through the wall of his ribs, and he lowered his hands to her hips to keep her from flying off as her speed increased. All too soon, Fargo felt the explosion building in him. He held back, however, waiting for Angelique to find her own release, and just when he thought he could resist no more, she threw back her head, openmouthed, and turned unseeing eyes to the sky.

"Now!" she said. "Now! Now! Now!"

Fargo let go, and the fiery stream shot from him like a geyser. Angelique bucked against him, biting down on her lip to keep from shouting her pleasure to the sky.

When it was over, Fargo leaned back against the side of the pool and watched the ripples still moving in the moonlight. Angelique drifted to his left and leaned back as well.

"It's been a while," she said. "Not that I haven't had offers aplenty."

"Harragan," Fargo said, as the warm waters of the spring soothed him from his exertions.

"Among others. But none of them was the kind of man I'm looking for."

"I'm afraid I'm not that man, either," Fargo said.

Angelique laughed. "Don't worry, Skye. I haven't set my cap for you."

Fargo nodded. "I didn't think you had."

And he hadn't. Angelique knew that he wasn't likely ever to settle down. He'd been cutting trails or following them most of his life, and he couldn't change now. Being in one place for more than a few days gave him itchy feet, and he had to leave, strike out for the mountains or the prairies, anywhere people didn't live in houses and build up towns. He'd stay in Hot Springs long enough to help out Angelique if he could, but whether he could or couldn't, he'd be gone before too long. He might come back for a visit someday, but that was all it would amount to.

"Nothing against you, Skye," Angelique said, breaking into his thoughts, "but I'm looking for someone who wants to settle down and run a saloon."

"Ought to be plenty of those around," Fargo said.

The chill of the night air was settling on his shoulders, and he ducked down under the water to ward it off. When he surfaced, he saw that Angelique had ducked herself as well. She shook water out of her hair and said, "Not as many as you think, and the ones I've met don't appeal to me in other ways."

"Harragan again."

"He's one of them. He's rich and ambitious, but there's something about him I don't like. And now he doesn't like me, either." She shivered, but Fargo didn't think it was from the cold. "Let's go back to the Traveler, Skye."

Fargo agreed, and they got out of the steaming pool. They dried themselves briskly with the towels Angelique had brought, rubbing until their skin was red. Then they dressed and walked back to the saloon, carrying the damp towels.

When they went inside, no one was there.

"Not one of our better nights," Angelique said. "If this trouble keeps up, I won't have any customers at all."

"I'll see what I can do," Fargo said.

"I'm sure you will, and I appreciate your help. Not just anybody would have come to help out an old friend without even knowing what the problem was."

"Always glad to be of service."

Angelique nudged him with her elbow. "Service? You certainly were of service. Do you think you might be up to it again?"

"Yes, ma'am, I think I might."

"Stop by my room first, then," Angelique said, "and we'll find out."

"Sounds like a good idea to me," Fargo said.

5

The next morning Fargo sat in the saloon drinking coffee and listening to the soiled doves talking about this and that, mostly their opinions of some man or other. Nothing they had to say flattered anybody.

Otherwise, the place was quiet. The piano man hadn't come in. Alfred was behind the bar, but he was sitting on a stool with nothing to do, so he'd laid out a hand of solitaire to see if he could hand old Sol a licking.

Fargo thought an easy day might lie ahead if things didn't pick up soon. Then Marshal Tatum shoved through the batwings and loomed in the entrance.

Tatum didn't say good morning. He said, "All right, Fargo, I warned you, and now I'm taking you in."

Fargo stood up. "I don't know why you'd want to start up with me this morning, but you're not taking me anywhere. What's your problem, Marshal?"

"My problem is that there's another dead man in town."

"I don't know anything about that. I haven't had time to kill anybody this morning."

"It was last night he was killed," Tatum said.

"I can tell you where I was last night."

"I bet you can. So can I. You were killing Steve Harragan's kid."

It took a lot to surprise Fargo, but Tatum's words did the trick.

"The hell you say."

"You don't have to look so damn surprised. I know you did it."

"I didn't kill Dave Harragan. Tell me what happened."

Tatum looked at Fargo. Something he saw must have convinced him not to push the murder charge at the moment. He said, "He drowned."

"Where?" Fargo said.

"You know where."

Fargo took a step toward Tatum, who drew his pistol.

"Stop right there, Fargo. I'm the law here, and don't you forget it."

"And this is my saloon," Angelique said, coming down the stairs. She was wrapped in a robe. Her hair was still tousled from the bed, but her blue eyes snapped. "I don't care if you are the law. You can't come in here pulling your gun."

"He says I killed Dave Harragan last night," Fargo said.

"I heard him. You should know better than that, Marshal. Why, we had supper with him last night."

"You don't have to tell me," Tatum said. "Plenty of folks saw you with him, but nobody saw him after that. Or you, either."

Angelique walked to Fargo, looped her arm around his, and leaned her head against his shoulder. "I can tell you where we were, Marshal. If you really want to know."

Tatum looked furious, and Fargo knew that he must have been one of the others Angelique had mentioned.

"I don't want to know," the marshal said.

"I'll tell you anyway. We were together. All night. If you're accusing Skye Fargo, you'll have to accuse me, too."

Tatum didn't seem to know whether to shit or go blind, so he holstered his pistol. "I'm not accusing you."

"Or Skye," Angelique said.

Tatum had to struggle, but he got the words said. "Or Fargo."

"Good," Fargo said. "Now tell me what happened."

"Couple of people went out to take a little dip in one of the springs this morning," Tatum said. "Found the Harragan kid was there already. Floating on top, dead. Drowned."

"An accident, maybe," Fargo said.

Again Tatum had to fight to get the words out. "Could've been an accident, maybe."

Or maybe not, Fargo thought, not believing it any more than Tatum did. "Where's the boy now?"

"Over at Carson's."

"I'd like to take a look at the place you found him."

"If you didn't kill him," Tatum said, "it ain't none of your business."

"He was a friend of mine. I saved his life on the trail. That makes it my business."

Tatum shrugged as if giving up. "To hell with it. Come on, Fargo. I'll take you."

Angelique slipped her arm from Fargo's. "Be careful, Skye" she said.

"You can count on that," the Trailsman told her.

Fargo was surprised again a short time later when Tatum said, "This is the place."

It was the same pool Fargo had visited with Angelique. There was no one in it now, and there wasn't likely to be for a while. People would bathe in other springs until they forgot about the drowning. Fargo looked around the edges for signs of what might have happened, but there was nothing he could see. There hadn't been a struggle on the bank. Either Dave had gone into the pool willingly or he'd already been unconscious when someone put him there.

"Guess it could have been an accident, all right," Tatum said when Fargo had finished his examination. "Kid could've come down before he went to bed. Maybe had too much to drink, and the heat got him so relaxed he just slipped under and drowned."

Fargo felt the back of his neck getting warm with anger. He didn't believe for a minute that Dave had drowned by accident. Since Fargo had an alibi and couldn't be arrested, Tatum wanted a simple answer, something he could tell Harragan when the hotel owner got back to town. If he couldn't give him Fargo as a killer, he'd give him an accident.

"That all you got to say about it?" Fargo asked.

"That's all. It's over, so you can forget about it. I'm sorry I accused you. My mistake. I can see now that it was just an accident. Kid shouldn't have come down here by himself after dark, maybe drunk. Fell in and couldn't get out. I hate to have to tell his pa, but that's my job."

Fargo wasn't going to forget it, but there was nothing to be gained by telling Tatum that. Tatum wouldn't understand all the reasons why, anyway.

It wasn't just that Fargo had saved Dave's life, though that figured into it. What made the difference to Fargo was that Dave had come looking for what was left of his family, and he'd been only hours from finding it. Fargo understood the kid's urge better than Tatum did. When Fargo was just a kid himself, he'd lost his own family and he'd spent his life wandering the West in the hope that

52

eventually he'd run across the people responsible. He couldn't have his family back, but he could make someone pay. It hadn't happened yet, but someday it might.

Now here was Dave Harragan, his mother dead, his father a rich man whom Dave hadn't seen in a few years. He'd been only hours away from seeing his pa again before somebody had robbed him of the chance. Somebody ought to pay for that, Fargo thought.

"You hear me, Fargo?" Tatum said. "You just forget about this. I'll handle it."

"I know you will," Fargo said. "I'll be getting on back to my job now."

"You do that."

Fargo didn't answer, and he didn't go back to the saloon. He went to Corby Carson's place. Carson was hammering together a coffin when Fargo walked up.

"Mornin', Fargo," Carson said, laying his hammer inside the empty box. "Killed anybody lately?"

"Not today," the Trailsman said, "but Tatum came by to accuse me of it."

"You mean the Harragan kid. I got him inside. Gotta plant him today, along with the two you did for last night. I tell you, Fargo, you've been a real boon to my business."

"I didn't mean to be. Things just happen, sometimes. I didn't kill Dave Harragan, though."

"I never said you did." Carson pulled out some tobacco and papers. "You want a smoke?"

"Thanks," Fargo said, "but I got my own."

"Careful where you throw a match," Carson said.

The ground was covered with fragrant pine shavings, and Fargo knew what would happen if any kind of fire got too close to them.

"I'm always careful," he said.

Carson nodded. "I figured that."

The two men rolled cigarettes and fired them up. Fargo snuffed his lucifer between thumb and finger and stuck it in a pocket.

Carson blew a perfect smoke ring and said, "You didn't come by here just to tell me you didn't kill Steve Harragan's kid, I bet."

"Nope," Fargo said. "I came to ask you what you knew about Marshal Tatum and Steven Harragan."

"Told you I don't know Steve too well. Don't know Tatum all that well, either."

"I didn't ask that. I asked what you knew *about* them."

"That's different, I guess," Carson said, blowing another smoke ring. "I don't know nothin' 'cept what I've heard, though."

"That'll do. Tell me what you've heard."

"I'll trade for you tellin' me why you're so interested in 'em."

Fargo thought it over. He couldn't see the harm in telling Carson about his interest. "You know most of it. Somebody tried to kill Dave yesterday and me last night. Now Dave's dead, and the marshal's going to call it an accident since he can't blame it on me. The marshal thinks it's none of my business, but I'd like to know what's going on."

Carson looked around. Fargo didn't see anybody, but Carson said, "Let's go inside."

They went into the barnlike building where the odor of pine tar was strong. Fargo cleared a space on the dirt floor and dropped his cigarette butt before crushing it out. Carson did the same.

"Harragan came here a couple of years or so ago," Carson said, leaning against the wall. "Had some kind of ailment in his leg, he said, and the waters in the spring healed it up in no time a'tall." Carson paused. "Didn't do his eye much good, though."

"Where'd he get the money to buy that hotel?"

"Well, he got it cheap. The owners didn't want to sell for a while, but things went bad for 'em. Seems like there was all kinds of trouble there not long after Harragan came to town. People gettin' sick after eatin' the food, rats in the rooms, fights startin' when people were havin' a meal, men gettin' drunk and goin' in the springs buck naked."

Fargo didn't have much to say about that, but then Carson had no way of knowing that Fargo had been in the springs. Besides, he hadn't been drunk.

That reminded Fargo of something else he wanted to ask Carson, but he thought it would wait until the old man had finished telling about Harragan.

"Even if he bought the place cheap," Fargo said, "he had to get the money from somewhere."

"Had the money all along. Said he won it gambling. Don't look like much of a gambler if you ask me, but nobody ever asks me."

"After he bought it, the trouble stopped, I take it."

"Sure did. Funny how that worked out. Now Harragan wants to buy that saloon Miss Angelique owns. Trouble's started there, too, I hear."

Carson said all this in a neutral tone, but it was easy enough to tell that he had some suspicions about what was going on.

"You think Harragan's behind the trouble at the saloon?"

Carson pushed himself away from the wall. "I'm just a carpenter and coffin maker. I don't get paid to do a lot of thinkin'."

He walked to the back of the building where two coffins rested on sawhorses. Beside them there was a board on which something else lay, something covered with a sheet of white cloth.

Fargo didn't press him any further about Steven Harragan. He changed the subject to what he'd been wondering about.

"Was Dave Harragan wearing any clothes when they brought him in?" he said.

Carson lifted the sheet. "Take a look for yourself. There he is, just the way he came in."

Fargo joined Carson and looked under the sheet. "Dressed the way he was the last time I saw him. Boots and all."

"That's right," Carson said, lowering the sheet. "But he drowned. Fella don't get in the water with his clothes on. Don't make sense."

"He might if he was drunk."

"Might," Carson said. "Might not."

"Yeah," Fargo said after a few seconds.

He lifted the cloth again and looked at Dave's body. There was a bruise on the side of his head. Fargo let the cover fall without mentioning the bruise.

"You got any more to say about Steven Harragan?"

Carson shrugged. "He does a good business at that hotel. He goes to church on Sunday."

"Sounds like an upright man," Fargo said. "He and the marshal are good friends, I guess."

"I wouldn't know 'bout that. They get along all right, far's I know."

"The marshal's a good man, too, I take it."

"You could say that."

"I know I could say it, but what about you?"

Carson walked back to the front of his shop. Fargo followed along.

"I came here about five years ago, Fargo," Carson said. "Had the bad lumbago in my back. Sometimes I wanted to cry like a little kid. Couldn't hardly straighten up. I spent a week in the springs and got downright spry again, so I decided to settle here. Got my own little business. I don't work too hard unless there's a lot of dyin', which there ain't, that is, not 'til just recently."

Fargo didn't know what any of this had to do with Hank Tatum, but he figured he'd let Carson tell things his own way. He'd get to the point eventually, or at least Fargo hoped he would.

"I still have to bathe in the springs once or twice a week," Carson continued, "else that lumbago'll come back and get me down again. I sure as to God don't want that. So you can see that I got to get along here. That means I got to get along with the marshal. With Harragan, too."

Now Fargo knew what Carson was getting at. "I'm not trying to cause you any trouble with either of them. I'm here to help out a friend, and now that Dave's dead, I'd like to know what happened to him. That's all. I'm not going to repeat anything you tell me. You can believe that."

"Oh, I believe it," Carson said. "I've heard of you, Trailsman. I know you're a man that keeps his word. Sometimes things get out, though."

"Not this time."

Carson didn't say anything for a full minute. He stroked his scraggly beard and stared out the open door at nothing at all.

"All right," he said at last. "I'll tell you this much. Tatum and Harragan might not be such good pals, but that's because both of 'em made a run at Miss Angelique and didn't do any good. Each one of 'em blames the other one for that. But even if they ain't friends, they get together and talk right regular."

"Talk about what?" Fargo wanted to know.

"I wouldn't know about that. I just happen to know they get together 'cause a lady who works at the hotel told me about it once. The two of 'em meet about once a week in Harragan's office, but Tatum comes in through the back door. Hardly anybody in town knows it."

Fargo thought that over. He didn't know what it meant. He didn't know much more than he had when Carson had started talking.

All he knew was that two men had tried to kill Dave Harragan for some reason. And two men had tried to kill him. All four of those men were dead now, and so was Dave.

"You want to hang around, it's all right with me," Carson said. "I got to finish this coffin box and get three men buried. With the two yesterday, I'm about worked out. You can lend a hand."

"I have a job," Fargo said.

"Better get to it then."

"You're right. I'll be seeing you, Corby."

Carson glanced back at the coffins. "I wouldn't be a bit surprised," he said.

Back at the Arkansas Traveler, business was picking up. It was still early in the day, and the real drinkers wouldn't start coming in until a bit after noon, Fargo figured, but several people were already at the bar, and a card game had started up. The piano player tinkled the keys, and the soiled doves were doing the best they could to work up some interest from a couple of men who looked as if they might have just arrived in town, trail dust still on their clothes.

Angelique came down the stairs and greeted Fargo almost as soon as he'd entered.

"What happened?" she said.

They sat at a table, and Fargo told her as briefly as he could. When he'd finished, he said, "There's a few things about all this that bother me. Aside from the obvious ones, I mean."

Angelique leaned her elbows on the table and asked what those not-so-obvious things were.

"Dave's clothes, for one. He was dressed. He didn't get in the water that way, no matter how drunk he was. And nobody could make him get in willingly."

"You don't believe he was drunk, do you?"

"No, I don't. I think somebody got him into that spring, but he might already have been dead by then. I saw the body. He wasn't shot, but he'd been hit in the head."

"Maybe he jumped in the water, hit his head on a rock, and drowned."

"Could be. That'd be the easy answer."

"And if it's not?"

"If it's not, somebody killed him. Or maybe he just bumped his head somewhere, wandered around in a daze and fell in the spring. I wish I knew."

"Knowing you, I'd say you intend to find out."

"I do," Fargo said. "I won't neglect my job here to do it, though."

Angelique reached out and touched his arm. "I know that, but even if you do, it's all right."

"Nothing's going to happen to this place while I'm in town."

"You might need help."

Fargo grinned. "You really think so?"

"No," Angelique said. "I don't."

6

The rest of the morning went by quickly and quietly as did most of the afternoon. Then a man came in and said he was looking for Fargo. Fargo got up from his chair in the back of the saloon and went to meet him.

"I'm Fargo. What can I do for you?"

"Mr. Harragan sent me over to ask if you'd come talk to him. It's about his son."

Fargo looked over at Angelique, who was sitting near the piano. She nodded, and Fargo told the man he'd be along in a little while.

"Mr. Harragan will be in his office," the man said. "First floor of the hotel."

"I'll find him," Fargo said.

When the man had left, Fargo walked over to Angelique's table and sat down.

"What do you think?" he said.

"You should go," Angelique told him. "He'll want to know about his son."

"I can't tell him much."

"Anything might help. He must be upset about what's happened."

Fargo wondered if that were true. Harragan hadn't

shown any interest in his son, or his wife, for that matter, in the last few years.

"I'll go," Fargo said, "but you send word if anything happens here."

Fargo didn't think Harragan would have anyone start trouble while Fargo was in his office. He didn't even know for sure that Harragan was behind the trouble. But he didn't want to take any chances.

"It'll be all right," Angelique said. "You go ahead."

Fargo stood up. "I'll be back as soon as I can."

"Don't worry." Angelique gave him a smile. "Things will be fine here."

Fargo hoped she was right.

The desk clerk directed Fargo to Harragan's office, which was in the back of the hotel. Fargo knocked on the door and entered when a voice inside told him to come in.

The office was as well furnished as one in a big city, Fargo thought. A big oak desk sat opposite the door, and heavy oak chairs faced it on either side. The wall behind the desk was covered by a bookshelf that held more books than Fargo had ever seen in one place, and he wondered if Harragan had read all of them. Or any of them.

Harragan stood up from his seat at the desk and walked around it to shake Fargo's hand. He was a large man and didn't much resemble his son. Of course the fact that he wore a dress suit and an eye patch might have had something to do with that. He was clean shaven, and his brown hair was long and combed back. Fargo noticed that he had no trace of a limp.

"You must be Fargo," Harragan said. He had a firm grip like that of a man who'd done some work with his hands. He released Fargo's hand and pulled back one of the heavy wooden chairs. "Please take a seat. Can I offer you a drink?"

"It's a little early for me," Fargo said. "You go ahead if you want to."

"I don't drink much, myself. I'd like to hear about my son. About Dave."

Fargo sat down while Harragan went back behind his desk. The Trailsman didn't like sitting inside little rooms to talk to men like Harragan, men who looked as if they hadn't spent much time outside. And while Harragan's office couldn't be described as little, it still gave Fargo a cramped feeling. He never got that feeling in a bedroom, for some reason. It must have had something to do with the differences in the situations.

"I'm sorry for your loss," Fargo said. "I didn't know Dave long, but he seemed like a fine young man."

"He was," Harragan said. He lowered his head and covered his eyes momentarily. "I can hardly believe he's gone."

Fargo didn't know what to say to that. It wasn't as if Harragan had let his family hear from him while he was in Hot Springs. Seemed to Fargo that the man had gone out of his way *not* to let them hear from him.

"I know you must think I'm a damn sorry excuse for a father and husband," Harragan said.

Fargo started to make a halfhearted protest, but Harragan stopped him by holding up a hand.

"No need to deny it. I know it's true, and I don't blame you a damn bit. Just tell me about Dave, and then I'll try to explain myself."

"You don't have to explain anything to me," Fargo said, though he hoped Harragan would indeed do some talking. Fargo wanted to get to know him a little, see what kind of man he was up against. "I happened to meet your son on the trail. Two men were trying to kill him, and I was able to help him out. I thought his troubles were over after we got to town, but apparently I was wrong."

"The marshal said you mentioned something about the men being paid to kill Dave."

Well, well. Tatum hadn't passed that information off as lightly as Fargo had thought.

"That's right. You got any idea why somebody would want to do that?"

"How do you know they weren't gunning for you? You were out there on the trail, same as Dave."

"I've thought about it," Fargo said. "It could be I was the target. A couple of men tried to kill me last night, too."

"I heard about that. Could've been just two drunks."

"Could've been," Fargo said. "Now tell me why someone would want to kill your son."

"Just tell me the rest of your story first, Fargo, and then maybe I can answer that question."

Fargo thought that would be a good trade, so he told him what he knew, which wasn't much and didn't take long. He did mention that Dave had been writing to his father but had never heard anything in return.

Harragan listened with a stricken look. When Fargo had finished, he said, "It's my fault. I should have sent for Dave and his mother long ago. I've been getting his letters, but I never felt the time was right for him and his mother to come. Now I know I was wrong. Anytime would have been better than this, but now it's too late."

Fargo wasn't sure how sending for Dave and his mother would have fit with Harragan's supposed advances to Angelique, but he refrained from asking.

"This is what happened," Harragan said, and he launched into his story.

As Dave had said, Harragan headed to Hot Springs

in hopes of a cure for his bad leg. The waters had worked what Harragan considered almost a miracle, and he'd been cured in only a couple of weeks.

"Not completely, though," he said. "I still have a little limp."

Fargo nodded, and Harragan went on with his tale.

When he wasn't soaking in the springs, he'd been playing cards in some of the saloons, and he'd been lucky enough to win a considerable sum of money, though he didn't say how much. The Grand came on the market about the time he was cured, the price was right, and he'd made the purchase.

"I didn't know a thing about running a hotel," Harragan said. "Still don't. But I hired a couple of people who did know, and I've been doing a right smart business ever since."

Fargo thought about asking how Harragan had gotten the place at a bargain, but Harragan saved him the trouble.

"Seems like my run of good luck at cards carried over to buying this place," Harragan continued. "The people who sold it were having some troubles, and they were anxious to get rid of the place."

"What sort of troubles?" Fargo asked, as if he hadn't heard the story before.

"Folks coming around and misbehaving, getting drunk and then abusing the people staying here, carrying on late at night, things like that. The owners hired some hard cases to put a stop to it, but that didn't work."

Fargo hadn't heard that part, so he asked Harragan about it.

"The drunks were harder than the hard cases," Harragan said. "Some of the hired hands got hurt. Before long, they left town."

"Sounds pretty serious," Fargo said.

"It was, and I was sorry to take advantage of it, but I couldn't pass up the chance to own this place."

He waved a hand around as if to take in the entire hotel with the gesture.

"It's a fine establishment," the Trailsman said. "I can see why a man would want to buy it."

The first part was true. The second part wasn't. Fargo had never wanted to own any property, no matter how grand it was. He'd never be tied down by owning things.

"You're probably wondering why I didn't send for my wife and son," Harragan said. "If this is such a fine place."

"It crossed my mind," Fargo admitted.

"I was worried," Harragan said. "The things that happened to the previous owners might start happening to me. You see, I think someone was behind the trouble, someone who wanted to buy the hotel."

"Now who'd want to do a thing like that?" Fargo asked.

"You don't have to sound so skeptical. It could happen."

Fargo didn't doubt it. The thing of it was, he thought Harragan had been behind the troubles.

"They might have hurt my family," Harragan said. "Dave. Lucy." He looked at Fargo. "That was my wife's name."

And now they're both dead, anyway, Fargo thought, though he didn't say it.

"I was just trying to protect them," Harragan said. "And I was right. Things have started to happen again here at the hotel."

Fargo had already been surprised twice by the marshal, and now Harragan had managed to do it.

"What things?" he said.

"I understand that you're a friend of Miss Leblanc,"

Harragan said. His tone said he didn't like the idea. "She could tell you."

"She's hired me to take care of some little things," Fargo said.

"Not so little, from what I've heard. Not unless you call those two dead men last night little." Harragan paused. "Maybe you'd like to go to work for me, too."

"You're having the same kind of trouble?"

"That's right."

Fargo hadn't heard a thing about that. Angelique hadn't mentioned it. Neither had Corby Carson nor the marshal.

"And you think somebody's trying to force you out?"

"I believe so. And that brings us to my son. To Dave." Harragan's face clouded. "I think whoever's causing the trouble had him killed. They must have been afraid he'd join forces with me and strike back at them."

"Seems like you could do that without any help," Fargo said. "You have law here in Hot Springs. It's Marshal Tatum's job to keep the peace."

Harragan leaned back in his chair. "He does a good enough job of it, too, most of the time, but he hasn't been able to do anything about my problems, or the ones Miss Leblanc is having. Oh, he can bust up a fight now and then, and he can clear the drunks out of the dining room, but he can't stop them from coming back. That's why I could use your help."

"Sorry to disappoint you, but I already have a job."

"I could pay you well."

"I'm working for a friend," Fargo said. "I don't do this kind of thing for money."

Harragan's eyes narrowed.

"You have any idea who's behind all this?" Fargo said.

"As a matter of fact," Harragan said, "I do."

*　　*　　*

Fargo went back to the Traveler a few minutes later with a lot to think about. He hardly noticed the people he passed along the way, hardly heard the barking of the dogs or the rattle of the wagons in the street.

Harragan had gone on to tell Fargo that he suspected a man named Clyde Brundage, the owner of the Superior Hotel, of being the one causing the trouble.

"He tried to buy this place before I did," Harragan said. "But the owners wouldn't sell to him, and I got it instead. He didn't seem all that upset, but I think he was just biding his time, letting me build up the business again, and then trying to force me out."

"You got any way to prove that?" Fargo wanted to know.

"No. If I could prove Brundage was behind things, maybe Marshal Tatum could do something about it. As it is, there's nothing to be done."

"Seems to me you're the one wanting to buy Miss Leblanc's place," Fargo said. "Not Brundage."

"You can ask her if Brundage's made an offer," Harragan said. He gave Fargo a bland look. "I just offered to buy her place to get her out of a difficult situation. A way to help her out, you might say. Like a friend would do." He emphasized the word *friend*. "I'm already dealing with the kind of thing that's happening at her saloon, and I figured maybe I could deal with both things at the same time."

Had Angelique been misleading Fargo? He wondered if there was more to her request than he'd thought, and he wondered even more about the two men who'd tried to kill him.

Fargo liked for things to be simple. He liked a straightforward job. Following a trail, leading some pilgrims from one place to another, those were the kinds of things he did best. It was too bad that he kept getting involved in complicated situations.

When he got back to the saloon, Fargo looked around. There were several customers, and the piano was tinkling a spirited tune. Fargo leaned on the bar and had Albert pour him a whiskey.

"You know what's going on around here, Albert?" Fargo asked when he'd downed the drink.

"I just tend the bar and try to stay out of trouble," Albert said. "I don't like shooting and fighting. I'm a quiet sort of a fella."

Angelique came downstairs and joined Fargo. Albert moved to the other end of the bar to give them some privacy.

"What did you find out?" Angelique said.

"I'm not sure," Fargo said. "Harragan had a lot to say, but I don't know that I learned much from it."

"The poor man's been through a lot. Going out of town, then coming back to find out his son's dead."

"So you feel sorry for him?"

"Yes. Even if he's making trouble for me, I do."

"He says he's not part of the problem. What do you know about Clyde Brundage?"

Angelique looked away. "Him," she said.

"Yeah, him. You forgot to mention him, I guess."

"I didn't forget." Angelique turned back to Fargo. "I just didn't say anything about him."

"I expect you had a good reason."

"It seemed good enough to me. You want to hear it?"

"Let's go sit at a table. Or go somewhere to get something to eat. I could use it."

"Not the Grand," Angelique said. "It's too expensive."

"I don't much want to go there, anyway," Fargo said. "How about the Superior?"

"Not there, either. We'll go to Ruth Ellis's boarding-house."

That was fine with Fargo, as long as he got something to eat. Angelique told Albert to keep an eye on things.

"Where'll you be?" Albert asked with a bit of a nervous quaver in his voice.

"Just down the street at Ruth's," Angelique said. "Send somebody after us if anything happens."

"I'll do that," Albert said.

Ruth's boardinghouse wasn't far from the saloon, but then nothing was very far from anything else in Hot Springs. The house was located a couple of blocks off the main street beside one of the smaller springs. There was no bathhouse, but anybody staying at the boarding-house had easy access to the steamy waters.

A couple of people walked past Fargo and Angel-ique and went up the wide steps onto the porch of the boardinghouse. They didn't speak to Fargo or Angel-ique. Once on the porch, they opened the door and went inside. Fargo heard loud talk that was shut off when the door closed. A sign hung from one of the porch pillars. It said ROOMS. MEALS. Simple and direct, just the way Fargo liked it.

"She always fixes plenty of food," Angelique said. "Lots of people eat here besides the boarders."

"I heard 'em," Fargo said.

He and Angelique followed the two men inside. They went down a short hall to a dining room on the right. Four long tables filled the room, and there weren't many empty seats. The noise was much louder than it had seemed from outside.

The tables were covered with bowls of potatoes, beans, and greens. Someone brought out a platter of fried steak and set it down on a table. Most of the meat disappeared almost at once, as everyone seemed to stick in a fork and pull a piece away.

The crowd was mostly men, and they were talking, eating, and ladling food, sometimes doing all three at once.

A rumpled, gray-haired woman appeared beside Fargo. "Just find a seat," she said, raising her voice so she could be heard over the din. "Hello, Angelique."

"Hello, Ruth. I think I see two empty chairs over there."

She and Fargo made their way to the chairs. Plates and utensils were already laid out.

"It's every man for himself," Angelique said as she and Fargo sat down.

"I'll manage just fine," Fargo said, and he did.

He and Angelique didn't talk much while they ate. It would have been next to impossible because of the noise, anyway, and Fargo preferred to concentrate on eating. Most of the conversation consisted of asking somebody to pass a bowl or platter that he couldn't reach for himself. The food was good, and Fargo was glad they'd come. He noticed that Angelique didn't eat much, however.

When he was pleasantly stuffed, he suggested that they leave and take a walk back to the saloon.

"We can talk on the way," he added.

Angelique nodded. On their way out, she told Ruth to put the meal on her bill. Ruth nodded, and that was that.

"Doesn't look like anybody wants to buy her out," Fargo said when they were outside.

"Too much work involved," Angelique said. "She has a nice location, though. Let's walk back this way, through the trees."

A breeze stirred the pines as they walked back in the direction of the saloon, and before they'd gone far, Angelique led Fargo off the path to a little clearing where a big flat rock sat under a tree. Pine straw covered the ground, and a few stray pine cones lay scattered nearby. The sun came through the trees and made patterns on the ground. Fargo and Angelique sat on the rock in silence for a minute or so.

"Tell me about Brundage," Fargo said, finally. "Tell me why you didn't mention him."

"I hated to get him mixed up in all this. I can't believe he's the one behind anything."

Something in her tone made Fargo suspicious. "Why not? Has he made you an offer for the saloon?"

"Yes and no."

Fargo didn't like that kind of answer. He could tell things were going to get even more complicated.

"He made you some other offers, too, maybe," Fargo said.

"Not exactly."

In spite of Angelique's evasions, Fargo thought he was starting to catch on.

"You like him, don't you? You don't want him to be the one responsible."

"We were going to be married," Angelique said.

Fargo was starting to lose track of the times he'd been surprised since arriving in Hot Springs.

"What happened?" he asked.

"He found out about Saint Louis."

"And he held that against you?"

"He thought I was just a smart businesswoman. He's a churchgoing man, and he wanted a wife who was like him. He thought he'd be getting one. I guess you could say I led him on."

Fargo thought Clyde Brundage was probably a fool, churchgoing man or not. Fargo had known a lot of women, and there were few better than Angelique, no matter what her past had been. It was nothing to be held against her. He said as much to Angelique.

"I'm glad you feel that way, Skye. But he didn't, and I don't really blame him."

"How do you know he didn't want to marry you just for the saloon?"

"A woman can tell."

Fargo wasn't so sure about that. In his experience women were just as likely as men to be blinded by love, or if not blinded, to see only what they wanted to see rather than to see things as they were. He thought there was more to the story than Angelique was telling, but he couldn't figure out what it might be.

"Who told him about Saint Louis?" he asked.

"I don't know, and I was too ashamed to ask. I would have told him, myself, when the time was right."

That was another way people fooled themselves, Fargo thought. It seemed like the time for the big revelation never arrived until it was too late.

"You didn't have anything to be ashamed of," Fargo said. He put his arm around Angelique and she nestled against him. "Brundage could be the one causing the trouble just to get back at you."

"He wouldn't do that."

Yes, he would, Fargo thought. That was just the way some people were, and he doubted that Brundage was any exception. And it was for damn sure that Harragan wouldn't have his own son killed, whereas Brundage might have had the boy murdered, if not because he wanted Harragan's hotel, then because of Harragan's "friendship" with Angelique.

"What about Harragan?" Fargo said. "You ever get close to marrying him?"

Angelique drew away from Fargo. "Good Lord, no.

72

I'd never consider a thing like that. He makes my blood run cold."

"Why?"

"It's just a feeling I get when I'm around him." She settled against Fargo once more. "Just the opposite of the way I feel around you."

Fargo felt a stirring in his buckskins. "We better be careful or we're going to scare the squirrels," he said.

Angelique laughed. "I'm not worried about the squirrels, but other people do come this way now and then." She stood up and pulled Fargo along with her. "Let's get back to the Traveler. I don't like to be away too long."

"I'm going to have to take some more time off this afternoon late," Fargo said. "You might want to, too."

"What for?" Angelique said.

"Got to go to a funeral," Fargo told her.

7

The afternoon passed quietly, and when it came time for the funeral, Angelique was ready to go, dressed in black and wearing a black hat with a veil. She even carried a small black parasol.

"You must go to a lot of funerals," Fargo said.

"Not many," Angelique said. "This is a quiet town, most of the time. I just like to have the right clothes for the occasion."

"I should've brought a churchgoing suit," Fargo said. He wore his buckskins, as he always did.

Angelique smiled. "You'd look mighty funny in a suit like that. It would be like dressing a grizzly for church."

Fargo laughed, and they left the Traveler with the now familiar admonition to Albert about sending for Fargo if anything happened. Angelique led Fargo to the local cemetery. It was in a natural clearing among the pines and located on a little hill not far out of town. Not far from the Grand, for that matter.

A small crowd had gathered by the time Fargo and Angelique got there. A man in a dark suit stood at the head of a newly dug grave. Fargo smelled the dank smell of the fresh-turned earth.

The man in the suit held a Bible, and Fargo assumed

he was a preacher. Harragan, also dressed in black, stood near him. The only other person Fargo recognized was Corby Carson, who wore a suit so old that Noah might have worn it on the ark.

Scattered throughout the crowd were some men that Fargo wondered about. They were no more dressed for the occasion than Fargo was, and they looked like they knew how to use the guns they wore.

Marshal Tatum was there, and he appeared to be looking the men over, too. Fargo hoped there wouldn't be trouble.

Angelique nudged Fargo. "There's Clyde Brundage," she whispered. "Standing not far from Harragan."

The man she spoke of had on a suit like the preacher and like Harragan. Also like Harragan, he held a hat in his hands. A nice-looking man, he looked to be around forty to Fargo, his hair just turning gray at the temples. He didn't look much like a troublemaker, but Fargo knew better than to let looks fool him. One of the coldest killers Fargo had ever encountered had looked like an angelic schoolboy.

Brundage raised his head and looked at Angelique. When he saw Fargo beside her, he turned away.

"He doesn't like me," Fargo said.

"Can you blame him?" Angelique said with a hint of mischief.

"He doesn't know about me and you."

"He can guess. He's heard about Saint Louis. He knows what kind of woman I am."

"The best kind," Fargo said. "Let's get a little closer so we can hear what the preacher has to say."

The preacher, as it turned out, didn't have much to say at all. He hadn't known Dave Harragan, and it seemed that no one, not even his father, had been able to supply any information about the youngster. So the preacher just said a few words that might have served for the death of any man who died too soon. Corby Carson and a couple of helpers lowered the coffin into the ground. The preacher read the twenty-third psalm, said a prayer, and that was that.

Or that would have been that had Steven Harragan and Clyde Brundage not had words.

Fargo couldn't hear what was said between them, but it was obvious that the men were becoming increasingly agitated. Harragan reached out and gave Brundage a push.

Brundage pushed back, and Harragan stumbled. He wasn't far from the edge of the grave, and for a second Fargo thought he might fall in.

Harragan teetered dangerously, then caught his balance. As soon as he did, he made a dive for Brundage. Before anyone could intervene the two men tangled and fell to the ground. Fargo thought he saw Brundage go for Harragan's good eye with a thumb, but he was too far away to be sure.

"Do something, Skye," Angelique said, but the Trailsman didn't want to get into it. Tatum started for the two men, and it was his job to straighten things out. As far as Fargo was concerned, the fight didn't have anything to do with him.

And then it did. Several of the men Fargo had suspected didn't belong at the funeral started to fight as well, and they were involving everybody in the crowd.

One of the men picked up a grave-digging shovel and swung it at Corby Carson, who managed to avoid being brained only because he fell down before the shovel could connect with his cranium.

Fargo liked the old man and didn't want to see him hurt, so when the man raised the shovel to bring it down on Carson's head, the Trailsman stepped in.

He grabbed the handle of the shovel at the top of the backswing and gave it a jerk. The rowdy holding the shovel didn't let go. He whirled around, pulling the shovel from Fargo's one-handed grip and swung it at Fargo. The man didn't go for Fargo's head, however. He swung it at Fargo's ankles, hoping to catch him off guard.

The blade sang through the air, but the trick didn't work. Fargo jumped over the blade and landed solidly on the ground just as the blade passed under his feet.

As soon as he planted his feet, Fargo punched the shoveler in the gut with his right hand. The man doubled over, air whooshing from him, and Fargo clubbed him on the side of the head with his left fist. The shovel fell from the man's limp fingers. He fell onto the pile of earth dug for the grave and lay as still as if he were a candidate for burial himself.

"Thanks, Fargo," Carson said, struggling to his feet and dusting his old suit. His eyes bugged. "Look out!"

Fargo turned at the warning and ducked under the fist of a man who'd gotten behind him and swung at his head. The man was so surprised he'd missed that he lost his balance. Fargo gave him a shove and he tumbled over onto his downed companion. To keep him there, Fargo kicked him in the jaw. The man's teeth clicked together and a couple of them broke. The man let out a loud moan and didn't move.

Looking around for Angelique, Fargo saw that she could take care of herself. One man made a grab for her, but she thrust her parasol forward and gave him a hard poke in the family jewels. The man howled and clutched himself. Angelique swung the parasol like a club and whipped him across the face. He collapsed, whimpering. Angelique gave him another slap across the face for good measure, then looked around to see if anyone else wanted to try something with her. Nobody did.

Plenty of people wanted to mix it up with Fargo, however. One man jumped on his back, knocking off his hat and driving him forward in the direction of Carson, who skipped nimbly out of the way with an agility that belied his years.

Two other men rushed over, and each of them grabbed one of Fargo's arms as he struggled to dislodge the man on his back. They pulled him and his rider as fast as they could toward the open grave.

Fargo tried to dig in his heels, but he couldn't get any traction. His momentum was too great and the ground was too slick. He couldn't even slow down, and when they reached the foot of the grave, the two men holding his arms yanked down. With the man still hanging on his back, Fargo plunged into the hole.

He landed with a crash atop the casket, and the weight of the man on his back forced the breath from his lungs. The man, however, wasn't bothered, and he took advantage of the chance to wrap his thick fingers around Fargo's neck to prevent him from taking in any more air.

He did a pretty fair job of it, too. In only seconds, Fargo felt his face heat up, and it seemed as if his head had started to swell, too.

The man squeezed tighter. Fargo tried to buck him off, but had no luck. His own hands were trapped beneath him. Sparks and stars pinwheeled before his eyes.

Fargo wondered if they'd bury him where he lay or dig another grave for him.

Then his attacker made a mistake. He leaned forward to get a little leverage and choke off the last of Fargo's air. Fargo felt the man's hot breath on the back of his head.

At that instant Fargo snapped his head back and smashed it into the man's face. Fargo felt the cartilage of the man's nose collapse, and blood ran into his hair.

The man yowled and released his hold on Fargo's neck. Fargo bucked him backward and scrambled to his knees while sucking rasping breaths into his ravaged throat.

He turned around. His assailant was also on his knees, leaning against the side of the grave and holding his cupped hands to his face. Blood ran between his fingers.

The Trailsman didn't feel a bit sorry for him. He hit him on his hands, flattening them onto his already broken nose. The man screamed like a ruptured panther. Fargo hit him again, and he fell forward, weeping and wailing. He might have been gnashing his teeth, too, for all Fargo knew.

Fargo pulled himself up and peered over the rim of the grave. The fighting was just about over, and most of the crowd of funeral-goers had scattered.

Clyde Brundage lay on the ground. Harragan stood over him, a pistol in his hand. While Fargo watched, Harragan aimed the pistol at Brundage's head.

Fargo shouted Harragan's name and vaulted out of the grave. Harragan was distracted by Fargo's yell and turned to see who'd called him.

When he saw it was Fargo, he returned his gaze to Brundage and thumbed back the pistol hammer.

Fargo jumped. He hit Harragan at the instant the pistol fired.

The bullet missed Brundage and plowed up dirt beside him. Harragan tumbled to his right, and Fargo went with him. By the time they hit the ground, Fargo had Harragan's wrist in both hands. Fargo twisted the wrist and slapped Harragan's hand on a rock. Harragan dropped the pistol, and Fargo rolled off him, reaching for the gun. His fingers closed around the grip, and he rolled again, coming to his feet with the pistol in his hand.

Harragan pushed himself to his hands and knees while Fargo looked around for Tatum. The marshal should have put a stop to what Harragan had been about to do, but he was nowhere to be seen.

Angelique stood by Corby Carson. When she saw that Fargo was safe, Angelique started toward him. Carson trailed along behind her.

"Give me my gun," Harragan said, rising to his feet. "I'm going to kill that son of a bitch."

"Maybe so," Fargo said, "but you won't do it today. I'll hold on to this gun for a while."

Harragan reached for the pistol. "Damn it, it's mine. Give it to me."

Fargo brushed aside Harragan's grasping hand and gave the pistol to Angelique, who had reached them. She took the gun and held it down by her side.

"Not today," Fargo repeated. "You're not going to kill anybody if I can help it." He looked at Carson. "Where's the marshal?"

Carson brushed his beard. "He took off after some of those fellas who started the fight."

"Seems to me Mr. Harragan started the fight," Fargo said. "Him and that man lying on the ground over there."

A couple of people had come to Brundage's aid. They were all that remained of the crowd, or at least all that remained upright. One man knelt beside Brundage and held his head up, while another stood by watching.

"The son of a bitch said he was glad my son was dead," Harragan said. "Give me the pistol, Angelique. He doesn't deserve to live."

Angelique made no move to hand over the gun. "That's not for you to say."

"She's right, Harragan," Fargo said. "I'll get somebody to bring your pistol to you later this evening. Right now, it's not a good idea for you to have it."

"Doesn't look like you'll need it," Carson said. "Brundage might be dead already."

"He's not dead," Harragan said. "I wish to hell he was, but I didn't hit him hard enough for that."

He looked at Angelique again, but she didn't give him any comfort. He turned and walked away.

Fargo watched him go. He didn't stop at the grave. He went past it and down the hill toward town.

"Not a very happy fella, is he?" Carson said.

"Maybe he has a reason not to be," Angelique said.

Fargo wasn't so sure. The two men with Brundage helped him to his feet, and Fargo went over to see how Brundage was doing.

"He'll be all right," one of the men said. "I think. Fell on a rock and got his head stove in pretty good. He's a little woozy right now."

Brundage said nothing. His eyes seemed unfocused, and he wasn't steady on his feet.

"Need any help to get him back to town?" Fargo asked.

"We can manage," the man said.

He and his companion stood on either side of Brundage and helped him walk. Brundage was none too steady on his feet, but Fargo thought he could make it to town.

"Best funeral I been to in years," Carson said as he watched them go. "Usually don't have that much fun even at a weddin'."

"Fun?" Fargo said. "You nearly got your head bashed with a shovel."

"Thanks to you, I didn't, though." Carson looked around. "Now where's my gravediggers got off to? I guess they cleared out with ever'body else."

He wasn't quite right about everybody else. The two men Fargo had laid out on the pile of dirt still lay there. One of them sat up and looked around. When he saw what was going on, he got up and took off at a shambling jog without attempting to rouse the man who'd been beside him.

Fargo went over to where his hat lay on the ground. He picked it up, brushed off the dirt, and settled it on his head.

"What about that 'un?" Carson said, jerking a thumb in the direction of the man on the dirt pile.

As if he'd heard Carson's voice, the man sat up.

"What the hell?" he said.

"You got hit," Carson said.

"Damn." The man stood and slapped at his clothes with his hands. "I'm leaving."

He took off at a run, and Fargo didn't try to stop him. When he was gone, no one was left in the cemetery other than Fargo, Angelique, and Carson. The sun had dropped down behind the pines, and long shadows fell across the graves.

"Don't reckon you'd help me fill in the hole, Fargo," Carson said. "Seein' as how it like to have been your grave, too."

"I have to go on back to the Traveler," Angelique said. "You can help out here if you want to, Fargo. I'll send for you if I need you." She held up Harragan's pistol. "I'll take this with me. I might be able to stop any trouble all by myself."

"Ever'body's too tired to cause any more trouble right now, I bet," Carson said.

"I hope they're thirsty," Angelique said.

She went down the hill, and as she passed the little fence that surrounded the cemetery a low moan came from Dave Harragan's grave.

Carson twitched as if someone had struck him between the shoulders and whirled around. As he did a bloody, mangled face appeared out of the grave.

"Oh, shit!" Carson said. "Shit! I swear to God I thought that boy was dead! It ain't none of my fault he got stuck in that box!"

Fargo shook his head. "That's not Dave Harragan. He's the one who put me in that grave. Good thing he came to before we covered him over."

Carson recovered his composure. "Looks a little worse for wear, you ask me."

"He must have hit his nose on something," Fargo said.

The man craned his neck and didn't see any help. He sank back down below the level of the ground.

"You gonna get him out of there?" Carson said. "I'd do it myself, only I'm so old and feeble."

"You're about as feeble as a yearling mule," Fargo said.

Carson shook his head. "I'm spry, but I'm not up to pullin' anybody out of a grave."

Fargo went to the side of the grave and looked down. The man sat on the coffin. He didn't look like much of a threat to anybody.

"You need a hand?" Fargo said.

The man looked up. "Could use one."

Fargo leaned down and offered his hand. The man took it and pulled himself up and out of the grave.

"No hard feelings," the man said. "I just got caught up in the fight."

"Sure," Fargo said.

The man nodded and shuffled away.

"Well," Carson said, "is that the last of 'em, or did you leave anybody else lyin' around here that you forgot to mention to me?"

Fargo grinned. "That's all, I think."

"Then are you gonna help me with the shovelin'?"

"Why not?" Fargo said.

*　*　*

That evening Angelique sent out for food from Ruth's boardinghouse, and she and Fargo ate in her room. When they were finished, they talked about what had happened at the funeral.

"You think Harragan was telling us the truth?" Fargo said.

"About Clyde being glad that his son was dead?" Angelique said.

"Yeah. From what you told me about Brundage, I wouldn't think he'd be the kind to think something like that, much less say it to Harragan."

"Clyde's a fine man, but you never know what somebody might say in certain situations."

"What about the fighting? You think Brundage was the one who started it?"

"It seemed to start about nothing," Angelique said.

That's what Fargo thought, too. The way Fargo remembered it, the fighting broke out almost as soon as Harragan and Brundage had tangled. And it had looked to Fargo as if Harragan had started things.

"Are you going to take Harragan's gun back to him?" Angelique asked.

"I guess I will. Now that he's had time to cool down, he won't be shooting anybody. Will he?"

"I don't know," Angelique said. "Sometimes I wonder about him. He's got a mean streak."

Fargo could vouch for that after Harragan's behavior at the cemetery. Mean and dangerous.

"What about the good Marshal Tatum?" Fargo said. "Seems like he disappeared right in the middle of things."

"He went after some of the troublemakers, or at least that's what he said. He yelled something and chased after them."

84

"I think I'd seen a couple of them before."

"Here in the Traveler," Angelique said. "Trouble-makers, every one of them. Now they've made some more trouble."

"You think the marshal has any of them in the jail?"

"I wouldn't count on it."

Fargo wouldn't count on it, either. He got up and went to the dresser. Harragan's pistol lay on top of it. Fargo took the gun and slipped it in his belt.

"You be careful," Angelique said.

"You can count on *that*," Fargo said.

8

Harragan didn't want to see Fargo, according to the desk clerk, who said that Harragan had been upset by the funeral and its aftermath and had asked not to be disturbed. Fargo didn't mind, and he handed the pistol over to the desk clerk, who promised to give it to Harragan when the hotel owner was feeling better. When Fargo left the hotel, he decided to stop by and see how Clyde Brundage was doing before heading back to the Traveler.

The Superior Hotel wasn't superior to the Grand. It wasn't even as grand. It was a nice enough place, however, and Fargo asked the clerk if he could see Brundage.

"He's indisposed," the clerk said.

He was a small, prissy man with rimless glasses and hair plastered down to his head, the kind of man Fargo would expect to use a word like *indisposed*.

"I'd like to talk to him," Fargo said.

The clerk looked Fargo up and down. It was clear that he didn't like what he saw. "I'm afraid that's quite impossible."

Fargo didn't see any point in arguing with the man, and he turned to leave.

"What seems to be the trouble, Lemuel?"

The voice belonged to a young woman who had walked into the lobby in time to overhear part of the conversation.

"Nothing at all, Miss Brundage," the clerk said. "This, uh, gentleman was just leaving."

"You were looking for my brother?" the woman asked.

Fargo figured that if he stayed in Hot Springs long enough, he'd get used to being surprised. Nobody had told him that Brundage had a sister. He wondered why Angelique had omitted to mention that little fact.

"If your brother's Clyde Brundage. My name's Skye Fargo."

The woman looked at Fargo with considerably more approval than Lemuel had.

"I'm Prudence Brundage," she said. "You can come with me."

"But, Miss Brundage," Lemuel said.

"It's all right, Lemuel. I'll take care of Mr. Fargo."

"Very well," Lemuel said. "If you say so."

"I do say so. Follow me, Mr. Fargo."

She was quite a woman, and Fargo was happy to do as she said. She was short, coming up only to Fargo's shoulder, but what he could see of her within the confines of her dress indicated that she was very well put together.

She went past the desk clerk into a small office and closed the door when Fargo entered after her.

The room held a desk with a chair behind it. There was no other chair. The office wasn't nearly as well-appointed as the one Harragan used.

Prudence sat in the chair behind the desk and looked at Fargo. Fargo removed his hat and looked back at her. She had a pleasant face, not beautiful, but pretty, with a wide mouth and blue eyes.

"So, Mr. Fargo, what do you want with my brother?"

"I was at the funeral this afternoon," Fargo said. "I wanted to know how Clyde was doing."

"I heard about you," Prudence said. "From the men who helped my brother get back here. They described you and said you saved Clyde's life."

"I just stepped in like anybody would have."

"But nobody else did."

"Steven Harragan doesn't like him," Fargo said.

"Harragan doesn't like anybody except that Angelique Leblanc."

Her voice sounded like Lemuel's did when he mentioned Fargo.

"You don't approve of her?" Fargo said.

"I didn't say that."

"But you don't."

"Let's just say I think my brother could have made a better choice."

Fargo wondered if Prudence had been the one who'd told Brundage about Angelique's past. And if she had, how she'd found out about it.

"Is your brother all right?" Fargo said to change the subject.

"He'll be all right. He got hit hard, but Dr. Allison came by and checked on him. If Clyde stays in bed for a few days, he should be fine."

"That's good news," Fargo said. "Would it be all right if I talked to him?"

"Why?"

"I have a couple of questions for him about the fight that broke out at the funeral. I'm trying to figure out how it got started."

"I should think that would be obvious," Prudence said. "Harragan insulted him and knocked him down."

"I believe you," Fargo said to be polite, "but I'd like to ask him, anyway."

Prudence stood up. "Very well. Come along."

The office had a back door. Prudence opened it and motioned Fargo through. He entered another room, much larger than the office. It was a bedroom lit by a lamp that sat on a chiffonier. Near the bed was a window in the wall. A man lay in the bed, but he raised up when Fargo entered.

"Prudence?" he said.

"Yes, Clyde. And you have a visitor, a man named Skye Fargo."

Brundage pushed himself into a sitting position and leaned back against the headboard. He peered at Fargo.

"You're the one they say saved me."

"I just knocked the gun away," Fargo said.

"You did more than that." Brundage paused. "I've heard about you. You're Angelique's friend."

"That's one way to put it," Prudence said.

"She's a fine woman," Fargo said, ignoring the sarcasm in Prudence's tone. "I came here to Hot Springs to give her a little help with her business."

"Lots of trouble there," Brundage said, his tone neutral.

"Tell you the truth, I've been wondering who was behind it," Fargo said.

"I thought everybody knew the answer to that. It's Harragan."

"He says not. He claims you're the one."

"He would. That doesn't mean it's true."

"No more than you saying he's the one."

"Don't you two start an argument," Prudence warned.

"I'm not starting anything," Fargo said. "Just saying."

"Look," Brundage said. "You were there this afternoon. You saw what Harragan did. He's after my place, and he's after Angelique's. Anybody can figure that out."

"Well, now, that's what I'd like to ask you about," Fargo said. "What exactly was it that you said to Harragan this afternoon that started the fight?"

"Me? I didn't say anything."

Brundage appeared agitated and made as if to get out of bed. Prudence went over and put a hand on his shoulder. Brundage sank back down, and Prudence gave Fargo a hard look.

"You're going to have to leave," she said. "You're getting Clyde too upset."

"I'm all right," Brundage said. "I just don't like to be accused of something I didn't do. It was Harragan who started the whole thing. You were there, Fargo. You saw it."

"I saw him push you," Fargo said. "I didn't hear what you said to him."

"I didn't say anything. He came over to me and said I was a son of a bitch for coming to the funeral after having his son killed."

"And you denied it."

"Of course I did. I didn't have his son killed. I didn't even know the boy. I was at the funeral out of respect to a fellow businessman, and then he said that to me. I couldn't believe it."

"So you said something back?"

"We had a few words. Then he shoved me. I don't remember much after that."

"It was quite a fight," Fargo said. "Who were all those men?"

"That's a good question," Brundage said. "I didn't know a one of them. I don't think they're from around here."

That fit with what Fargo thought. He wondered where

they'd come from. More than that, he wondered why they were in Hot Springs, other than to make trouble.

"So they don't work for you or stay in your hotel?" Fargo said.

"Of course not," Brundage said. "We don't encourage people like that to stay here. There are other places."

"Like the Grand."

Brundage managed a weak laugh. "Hardly. Harragan might be a ruffian himself, but he wouldn't want that kind in his place. He likes families and people with money."

"He claims he's had some trouble there, drunkards scaring his guests. He blames you."

Brundage didn't try to rise. He just said, "He's a liar, then."

"I think it's time for you to go, Mr. Fargo," Prudence said. "You've tired Clyde out. He needs to rest."

"Just one more thing," Fargo said. "Harragan also said you were causing the trouble at the Arkansas Traveler."

"We've established that he's a liar," Brundage said. "I don't know what else I can tell you."

"You can't tell him anything else," Prudence said. "I'll show Mr. Fargo out."

Fargo didn't protest. He thought they'd go back out through the office, but there was a second door to the room, and Prudence went out through that one.

"This way, Mr. Fargo," she said.

The door opened into a hallway, and instead of turning to the front, Prudence led Fargo toward the rear of the building. When they reached the end of the hallway, she opened another door and went inside a room.

"You can come in," she said to Fargo when he hesitated.

Fargo wasn't sure going inside the room was a good

idea, but he still had a few questions that hadn't been answered. He hoped Prudence could answer them.

"There's nothing to be afraid of," Prudence said, as he walked in. "I won't hurt you."

"I didn't think you would," Fargo said.

The room itself made him uncomfortable, however. It was small, all pink and blue ruffles and flourishes, with a bed that had a fancy carved headboard that Fargo thought must have been shipped from somewhere back east.

"Please sit down," Prudence said. "We need to talk."

The two chairs in the room had fat stuffed seats and thin legs. They were fine for a small woman like Prudence, but Fargo wasn't so sure they'd hold a big man like him.

"The chairs are quite sturdy," Prudence said, as if sensing his doubts.

Fargo eased himself down on one of them. It was sturdy all right. It didn't make a squeak when he settled his weight on it. Fargo put his hat on his knee and waited to see what came next.

Prudence pulled the other chair near him and sat down in front of him so that their knees were almost touching.

"You seem awfully interested in my brother," she said.

"I'm a curious fella," Fargo told her.

"Oh, I think it goes beyond curiosity. It goes beyond the . . . job you're here to do for Miss Leblanc, too."

"Nope. I'm just trying to keep things peaceful at the Traveler. That's my job, and that's all I care about."

"You wouldn't have acted the way you did at the funeral if you were so uninterested. Why don't you tell me what's going on."

"Not a thing," Fargo said. "Except that I'm curious, like I said. Maybe you could answer a question for me."

"That depends on the question."

"Did your brother know that Dave Harragan was on the way to town to see his pa?"

Prudence looked thoughtful. "I don't think so. Why?"

"I wondered if Harragan had told anybody. Looks like he'd have been happy that his son was coming to see him, but he wasn't even in town when the kid got here."

"He goes out of town on business now and then. It was probably something he couldn't change." She leaned forward and put a hand on Fargo's leg. "Why are you so interested in Dave Harragan, anyway?"

"I didn't know him long," Fargo said, "but I liked him. I'd kind of like to know who killed him."

"But what good would it do you to find that out?"

"Maybe none."

Prudence removed her hand and regarded him seriously. "I know your kind, Fargo. You think you owe something to the boy. You can't let it go."

"Harragan won't let it go, either," Fargo said.

"He might. He has nothing to gain by pursuing it. And neither do you."

Fargo couldn't explain himself any better than he had already and he figured even a rotten father would want to know who killed his son.

"Doesn't look like Marshal Tatum thinks he has anything to gain, either," he said. "Looks like he'd want to know who killed Harragan's son or hired those men on the trail."

"The men weren't killed in town. He's not paid to handle things that happen way out on the trail. I admit Harragan's son is another story."

"Lots of other things have happened in town. The marshal doesn't seem real interested in those, either."

"We've had some trouble here at the hotel, too, you know."

"Seems like there's trouble all over," Fargo said. "I wonder why."

"You wonder too much." Prudence leaned close to him again. "I like you, Mr. Fargo. You saved my brother's life, and I'd hate to see anything happen to you."

"You don't have to worry about me," Fargo assured her.

"What about me?" Prudence said, leaning even closer. "Would you protect me?"

Fargo took in the clean smell of her blond hair along with the faint scent of perfume that rose from her dress and the cleavage of her breasts.

"If you needed protection, and I was around," he said, "you could count on me."

"I thought so," Prudence said, and she kissed him.

It wasn't a polite peck on the cheek. It was a deep, burning kiss, and when Prudence's tongue slipped between Fargo's lips, he suddenly lost all interest in the town, its troubles, and even Dave Harragan. He had much more immediate things on his mind.

The next thing Fargo knew, he and Prudence lay buck naked on the bed with the fancy headboard. Prudence moaned in delight as Fargo's fingers stroked her stomach and his tongue teased the tips of her breasts.

It had happened so quickly that Fargo didn't even remember removing his clothes. For that matter, he wasn't sure whether he'd taken them off or Prudence had, not that it mattered in the least. At the moment nothing much mattered to him other than the fact that Prudence was quite interested in the iron-hard shaft of his manhood. Her fingers played with the tip and slid up and down it as she lounged beside him.

She put a hand on his chest and gave a light push. Fargo rolled over onto his back, and Prudence leaned over him. The hot tips of her breasts blazed a trail down his stomach as she bent to kiss the tip of his rigid pole.

"Ummmm," she said, and took him into her mouth.

Using her tongue and mouth and occasionally her hand, she caressed him to the point of near explosion.

But Prudence was too experienced to let anything happen before she was ready. She stopped what she was doing and twisted around to straddle Fargo, positioning the opening of her sex just above the tip of his erect rod. She lowered herself slowly, and when Fargo felt the tickle of her pubic hair, he took hold of her hips, pulling her down at the same moment he thrust upward, slipping into her slickness with ease.

Prudence gasped as his thick member filled the fiery chamber, and Fargo twisted her hips to encourage her to rub herself against him.

"Oh," she said as she did. "Oh. Oh, my God!"

Fargo was in control now, and he slipped a finger between them to rub the sensitive bud that sat atop her sex.

"Ahhh!" she said. "Ahhhhh!"

She moaned in pleasure and delight as her climax shook her. It seemed to ripple up and down her body, and then she collapsed on Fargo's chest. He let her lie there for a moment to catch her breath. Then he began to move, withdrawing from her, then entering her again a little at a time.

Prudence was immediately aroused again. Her hips pumped as she met Fargo's thrusts, and he withdrew more and more with each one, plunging back inside her as deeply as he could.

Prudence sat up and took Fargo's hands, placing them on the firm globes of her breasts, encouraging him to squeeze them and fondle the stiff nipples. She rode him harder, and Fargo could feel the sap rising within him, ready to spew out like lava.

But he wasn't ready yet. He took a firm hold of her sides and rolled over until he was on top. He withdrew his member almost entirely, leaving only the tip inside her. Prudence opened her eyes and stared into his.

"I'm ready now, Fargo. I can't wait. Please. Give it to me. All of it. Now!"

Fargo held back for a second that seemed an eternity before sliding his full length into her, again and again. She churned wildly beneath him, her legs thrashing in the air.

After uncounted moments, she cried out and clasped Fargo in the strong grip of her crossed legs, holding him to her as his own climax wracked him. The stream burned out of him and into her as he groaned like a studhorse.

And then it was over. Fargo rolled off Prudence and lay quietly beside her as they caught their breath.

After a while Prudence said, "You're much of a man, Fargo. More than anybody I've known."

"And you're a hell of a woman," Fargo said.

It was the truth. She was so good at what they'd been doing that he wondered where she'd learned it all. It wouldn't, however, be polite to ask.

"You're Angelique's friend," Prudence said. "I know that."

"We've been friends a good while. She knows me pretty well."

"That doesn't mean she'd like knowing about what just happened. You won't tell her, will you?"

Fargo wasn't loco. "I don't kiss and tell."

"You have to worry, though, if she finds out."

"She might be mad, but it won't last."

"That's what you think."

Fargo wondered if Prudence was more worried about Angelique's feelings toward her or toward him.

"I can keep a secret," he said.

"Good," Prudence said. She half turned and let her

fingers travel down his stomach toward his manhood, which stirred slightly.

"You don't have to leave yet, do you?" she said.

"No," Fargo said. "Not yet."

Fargo hadn't intended to be gone from the Traveler for so long, but when he returned, he could see that he hadn't been needed. Things were going smoothly. More people were inside than there had been the previous evening, the piano music was a little louder, the soiled doves a little more boisterous, the gamblers a little more intent on their games.

Fargo went over to the bar.

"Looks like a good evening," he said to Albert.

"It is," Albert said. "Whiskey? You look like you could use one."

"I do?" Fargo said.

"Well," Albert said, reaching for a bottle of the good stuff from beneath the bar, "you've had a hard day, after all."

"I have?" Fargo said.

Albert poured Fargo a stiff drink. "I heard what happened at the funeral. And then you had to fill in the grave. That's strenuous work."

"Right," Fargo said. He downed half the glass of whiskey.

"You still look a little out of breath," Albert said.

"Strenuous work," Fargo said. "You know how it is."

"I try to avoid that kind of thing."

"Don't blame you." Fargo finished the whiskey. "Where's Miss Leblanc?"

"She's gone to her room. She said to ask you to stop by when you got in. She has something to discuss with you."

"Thanks," Fargo said. "I'll go up and see her now."

"Want another drink first?"

Fargo thought it over. "No, thanks," he said.

In spite of what he'd told Albert, Fargo didn't go directly up to Angelique's room. Instead, he stopped at one of the tables where the cards were being dealt. He waited until the hand was over and then pulled up a chair to sit in.

"You want me to deal you in?" one of the men at the table said as he shuffled the cards with thin, practiced fingers.

The man had bushy eyebrows and black eyes hard as the chips in the pile in front of him. It was a good-sized pile, and it indicated to Fargo that when it came to cards, the man was good at more than just shuffling.

"Just wanted to talk," Fargo said.

He had no intention of sitting in, though he was a pretty good cardplayer himself, having played in a big tournament in New Orleans at one time.

"Got no time for talkin'," another man said.

He wore rough work clothes and had only a small stake. He was either in a hurry to lose the rest of it or win some back, which in his case probably amounted to the same thing.

"Won't take long," Fargo said. "I was hoping one of you fellas could tell me a little something about Steven Harragan."

"Steve? The fella that owns the Grand?" a third man asked.

"That's the one," Fargo said.

"Why'd we know anything about him?"

"Supposed to be quite a gambler," Fargo said. "Lucky one, too. I thought maybe you'd heard about him or played in a game with him."

"Ain't ever seen him turn over a card," the first man said. "Least not since he bought that hotel."

"How about before then? I heard he gambled a good bit when he first hit town."

"He did," the second man said. "Wasn't much good at it. Sorry to go against what you said, but it's the truth. No offense."

"None taken," Fargo said.

"Truth is," the man went on, "he wasn't much better than I am." He waved a hand at the little pile of chips in front of him. "And you can see I'm no damn good at all."

"He's right about that," the third man said. "Both parts of it. Harragan couldn't play a lick."

"Well, now," Fargo said. "That's mighty interesting."

"Not to me," the first man said. "You want me to deal you in or not?"

"Not," Fargo said. He stood up. "I appreciate you taking the time to talk to me. You can go on and get back to your game now."

The first man was already dealing the cards. Neither he nor the other men even looked up as Fargo walked away.

He climbed the stairs and went to Angelique's room. He tapped on the door and entered when she told him to come in.

Angelique sat waiting for him. Her dark hair tumbled down and covered the shoulders of the thin white cotton gown she wore. It was obvious that she wore nothing under the gown.

"It took you longer than I thought it would," she said.

Fargo removed his hat. "Harragan didn't want to see me, so I stopped by to talk to Brundage."

"Why?"

"I had some questions about Harragan I thought maybe he could answer. And I wanted to see how he was doing."

"Did he answer the questions?"

"Not all of them. He's not feeling too pert. I did find out something, though."

"What would that be?"

"I found out he had a sister."

"Prudence," Angelique said. She looked as if she'd smelled something bad.

"That's her," Fargo said. "Nice name."

"It doesn't suit her," Angelique said.

Fargo didn't ask what name Angelique thought might have been better. He said, "What do you have against her?"

"You mean besides the fact that she's a scheming little bitch?"

Fargo thought it was no wonder Prudence hadn't wanted Angelique to find out about what had just transpired in the Superior Hotel.

"Besides that," Fargo said.

"I don't like to talk about her," Angelique said. "I guess it's because I think she's the one who broke up me and Clyde."

"I thought that was Harragan."

"It might have been, but Prudence is more likely."

"She told him about Saint Louis?"

"I think she was the one."

"What was her reason?"

"She hates me. She hates anybody that might come between her and Clyde. She controls him. Everybody knows that. She's really the one who runs the hotel. Clyde lets her, and she's afraid that someone will come along and give him a little backbone."

"You'd be someone who'd do that, all right," Fargo said.

"I sure would. Then Prudence would have to step aside. But now I'll never get the chance to make it happen."

"You never know."

"I know," Angelique said. "So let's not talk about Prudence." She ran her hands over her breasts, and Fargo saw her nipples stiffen and push out the fabric. "There are other things we could be doing."

Fargo smiled. "We sure could. Let me go clean up a little bit. I got dirty filling in that grave."

"You'll come back?"

"I'll come back," Fargo said. "You can count on me."

He thought about the last time he'd said that and smiled again.

Fargo sat in his room a few minutes later. He had washed up, but he wasn't ready to visit Angelique again, not yet. He had a lot to think about. Too many things he'd heard and seen since he got to Hot Springs didn't add up, and he wanted to see if he could get them straight in his mind.

He couldn't quite do it. Everything spun around like feathers flying out of an old pillow whirled in the air, but nothing settled to the ground in any pattern that he could make sense of.

He gave it up after a while and went back to Angelique's room. She still sat in the chair and still wore the nightgown.

"Took you a while," she said. "You must've gotten really clean."

"I did," Fargo said, and he wondered if she suspected he'd washed off more than the dirt from the cemetery. "Do you have any idea what part of the country the Brundages came from?"

"Clyde told me once that they'd lived most of their lives in the East. I believe he said Pennsylvania."

"How'd they wind up here?"

"I don't know. I believe there was some kind of family disagreement. Their father was a minister, and while Clyde's a good churchgoer, they must have had some kind of falling-out." Angelique looked at Fargo. "Did you really come here to talk about the Brundages?"

"Nope," Fargo said. "Just curious."

Angelique ran her hands over her breasts, caressing the nipples that poked against the fabric.

"Well, then. What did you come here for?"

"You'll see," Fargo said.

"I will? Then show me."

So he did.

9

Fargo slept like a stone that night after leaving Angelique's room. When he got up the next morning, Angelique was still in her room, asleep he guessed, maybe a little tired from the night's exertions. Fargo felt just fine, himself, but he was hungry and needed breakfast. He went downstairs to see if anyone was there.

Albert was already behind the bar to get ready for the day ahead, but otherwise the place was deserted. The gamblers were gone, and so was the piano man. The soiled doves were all in bed, either asleep or earning some cash.

"Be plenty of people in later," Albert said. "It's early yet."

Fargo acknowledged that it was and asked if the boardinghouse served breakfast.

"Sure does," Albert said. "A good one, too. It's usually pretty crowded." He looked around the saloon. "A lot more crowded than we are at this time of the day."

Fargo didn't mind a crowd as long as the food was hot and substantial. He told Albert he'd be back and headed for the boardinghouse.

Ruth greeted him at the door. "Go on in and find you a seat, if you can. Angelique said if you came back without her that you were eatin' on her bill."

Fargo nodded, thanked her, and went on inside, where the noisy diners were shoveling in eggs, bacon, sausage, grits, gravy, biscuits, butter, and anything else that came to hand. Fargo sat down in an empty chair at one of the tables, but nobody paid him any mind. Everyone was too busy eating.

That suited Fargo fine. He didn't want to talk. He wanted to eat, and that was exactly what he did.

After he'd finished, he pushed back from the table and left. He didn't go back to the Traveler but headed instead toward Corby Carson's place of business.

Fargo heard the sound of a saw as he approached, and the smell of fresh sawdust filled the air when he went into the barnlike building.

Carson stood just inside the door. He'd stopped sawing and was smoothing a plank with a plane. The curly shavings fell to the ground as he worked.

"Hey, Fargo," Carson said. "I'm working on another casket. Never know when I'll need one or two, what with you in town and shootin' folks."

"I haven't shot anybody today," Fargo pointed out.

"Maybe not," Carson said, "but it's early yet."

Carson took off his hat and wiped his brow with an old bandanna that he pulled from his back pocket. "I'm makin' this one to fit a six-foot man, so try not to kill anyone taller," he said as he returned the bandanna and went back to his planing.

Fargo shook his head not knowing what to reply to that. He rolled a smoke and watched him work for a couple of minutes.

"That all you got to do?" Carson said after a while. "Stand around and watch an old man work?"

"Seems like as good a way as any to pass the time," Fargo told him.

"Yeah. 'Bout as much fun as watchin' the grass grow. What's on your mind, Fargo?"

"Maybe I just dropped by to see how you were doing."

"You'd be the first that ever did, then. Nobody drops around to see about me. You got something you want to talk about, let's get on with it."

Fargo tossed Carson his makings. "Roll yourself a smoke first."

"Don't mind if I do," Carson said. When he was done, he tossed the makings back to Fargo. "All right. Now tell me what you came for."

"There's something funny going on in this town," Fargo said.

"Do tell. When did you notice?"

"Pretty soon after I got here. Tell me about the marshal."

Carson inhaled and blew out a stream of smoke. "Hank Tatum."

"Yeah," Fargo said. "I know his name."

"Came here not too long after Steve Harragan. Town hadn't had much law up till then. Didn't need much, come to think of it. Nice quiet little place."

"Trouble started after Harragan showed up?"

"Seems like that. And then Tatum came along, lookin' to do some lawin'. Seemed like he could handle trouble, so he got himself hired."

"And what kind of job has he done?"

"Pretty good," Carson said. He threw his cigarette butt on the ground and mashed it out.

"Just pretty good?" Fargo said. "What does that mean?"

Carson picked up his plane and checked the edge with his thumb. He seemed satisfied that it was still sharp.

"Means some people get better protected than others do," he said.

"Like Harragan?"

"Yeah, but then maybe he needs it."

"How come he needs it?"

"'Cause he has trouble at that hotel of his now and then."

"Like Miss Leblanc's having now?"

"That kind, yeah."

Fargo leaned against the wall and tilted his hat back. "You sure don't give a fella much to chew on."

Carson set down the plane. "Look here, Fargo, I like you. You're a nice enough fella, but you're not here to stay. You're just passin' through. I ain't got nowhere to go."

"What you tell me won't get spread around."

"Hell, I know that. The thing is, I don't know what's goin' on any more than you do."

"You live here, though. You have some ideas."

Carson thought about it. "Okay," he said after a while, "here's how it is. Harragan comes in here and buys the best hotel in town. He has some trouble, claims Brundage is behind it. Your friend, Miss Leblanc, she starts having some trouble, too. She thinks Harragan's behind it. I don't know which way it is, myself."

"Brundage claims to've had some trouble, himself."

Carson shrugged. "Very damn little, if you ask me."

"No matter how much trouble there's been," Fargo said, "Marshal Tatum's kept things from getting out of hand."

"Guess you could say that."

They talked for a while longer, but Fargo couldn't get anything more out of the old man. He really hadn't learned much, anyway. Things were pretty mixed up, and Fargo didn't see any way to sort them out.

On his way back to the Traveler, he made another detour and stopped at the jail. Tatum was there, sitting in a tilted-back chair, his booted feet propped up on the scarred desk in front of him. The walls of the jail were bare wood, though the cellblock was made of stone. The desk was bare, too.

"Howdy, Fargo," Tatum said. He made no move to get up. "You got a need for a little help from the law?"

"Nope," Fargo said. "I just wanted to see if you caught up to any of those troublemakers from yesterday."

Tatum swung his legs off the desk and leaned forward as his chair clumped down on the wooden floor.

"Didn't catch a one of 'em. They all got clean away. But I'll get 'em sooner or later."

Fargo thought it would probably be a lot later. He said, "Looked to me like Brundage and Harragan don't much like each other."

"Maybe not," Tatum said. "Is it any business of yours, one way or the other?"

"It is if it affects Miss Leblanc."

Tatum leaned back in his chair and clasped his hands over his belt buckle. "What're you gettin' at, Fargo?"

"I want to know who's causing the trouble here in Hot Springs, and I want to put a stop to it."

"Hell, Fargo, that's my job. You lookin' to take my badge away from me?"

"I don't want your badge," Fargo said. "I want Miss Leblanc's saloon to be a peaceful place where people don't get beat up or shot up."

"I'm doin' the best I can."

"For Harragan."

Tatum grinned. It wasn't a pleasant grin. "Where'd you get that idea?"

"Just seems that way to me, I guess."

"Well, it's wrong. Let me tell you something, Fargo, I

work for the whole town, not just Harragan. It's just that Harragan's got more troubles than most. He buried his kid yesterday. That's a hell of a thing."

"You got any idea who might have killed Dave?"

"Yeah, I got an idea. I figure Clyde Brundage had it done. He's the one causing the trouble around here. I just haven't caught him at it yet."

Harragan thought the same thing. It was beginning to look as if he might be right.

"Why would Brundage do a thing like that?" Fargo said.

"Maybe he didn't want Harragan to have another gun on his side."

"Looks like somebody has plenty of guns already."

"Brundage. But they're smart, and they're careful. They haven't killed anybody yet." He gave Fargo a hard look. "Somebody's killed plenty of *them*, though."

"Self-defense," Fargo said.

"In the eyes of the law. Their friends might not feel the same way."

He had a point, but so far nobody had tried to bushwhack Fargo. He didn't think they were the kind of men who'd confront him in a fair fight. He regretted he hadn't stopped one of the men he'd knocked around in the cemetery for a heart-to-heart talk.

"I'd watch myself if I was you, Fargo," Tatum said. "Now if you don't have anything else you want to talk to me about, I think I'll take a walk around town and see what's goin' on. That's what they pay me for."

Fargo nodded, thanked Tatum for his time, and left. As he did, he saw that Tatum was right behind him. The marshal closed the door and went to the left. Fargo turned right and headed back to the Traveler. He took his time. It was a nice day, and the smell of the pines from the mountains drifted down into the town and mingled with the odor of horse manure in the streets. Fargo thought about the springs and figured it might be a good idea to have another bath in them soon, though maybe not as strenuous as his earlier one with Angelique.

Fargo loitered along. He didn't know any of the people on the street, but he thought a couple of the men looked familiar. He couldn't swear that he'd seen them at the cemetery, but he thought he might have.

As he neared the saloon, Fargo saw three men go inside. This time he was certain he knew them. He'd seen at least one of them fighting among the graves. A fourth man stood outside the batwing doors and leaned on the wall, one foot up and propped against it. He looked up and down the street, but before he could see Fargo, the Trailsman ducked into an alley.

There wasn't much doubt that the men who'd gone into the Traveler were up to some mischief, and they'd left one man outside to watch for the marshal or Fargo or both.

Fargo wasn't going to be caught that easily. He slipped down the alley, and when he reached the back of the buildings, he turned to his right and went down that alley for a couple of blocks. Then he went back to the street, crossed it, and started for the Traveler.

Fargo's plan was simple. He'd go in through the back door and catch the men by surprise. There were at least three of them, but even if there were a couple more than that, he didn't think they'd stand a chance against him and his .44.

The back door of the Traveler was at the top of a couple of wooden steps. Fargo looked in both directions. He didn't see anyone in the alley. He drew his pistol and opened the door, and for the third or fourth time since he'd arrived in Hot Springs—Fargo was losing count—he got a surprise.

They were waiting for him.

Or rather one of them was, one that Fargo hadn't known about. When Fargo stepped through the door and entered the building, a man who'd been hidden behind the door moved out, stuck a cold pistol barrel against the back of Fargo's neck and said, "I'm going to reach around and take that pistol of yours. You make a wiggle, and I'll blow a hole in your neck so big a crow could fly through it."

"Be a mighty big hole," Fargo said. "Might be bigger than my neck."

"Then your head'd be sittin' flat down on your shoulders and you wouldn't have no neck at all. You gonna give up that gun or you want me to pull the trigger?"

Fargo didn't see any reason not to give up the pistol, especially since the three other gunmen in the saloon had their pistols out and pointed at Angelique, Albert, and Sam Hawkins, the piano man.

Angelique sat at a table, and Albert stood behind the bar. Hawkins sat on his piano bench with his back to the keys. He looked at Fargo and shrugged.

Angelique's face was stony and gave nothing away. Albert looked scared, but that didn't mean he was.

While Fargo stood there, the man from the front came inside. He had a pistol, too.

"Well, Fargo?" said the man at his back.

"Take the gun," Fargo said, letting the pistol hang loose from one of his fingers.

The man reached around Fargo, and in doing so he had to move just enough so that his pistol barrel was no longer touching Fargo's neck. The instant that the barrel moved, Fargo flipped his pistol back into his grip, whirling at the same time.

He grabbed the front of the man's shirt and slammed the barrel of his .44 into the man's head. The man's pistol went off, firing a bullet into the balcony floor above them, but the noise didn't slow Fargo. He continued his turn, holding the man in front of him with his back to the room.

Shots exploded. The man shuddered as bullets struck him. He sagged, and Fargo threw the body forward as hard as he could, diving forward himself. He hit the floor and rolled. Bullets whipped over his head. Others chewed splinters from the planks in the floor, and Fargo came up shooting.

A lot of things happened all at once. The first bullet that roared out of the .44 hit the man who'd been outside. He stopped in his tracks and crumpled to the floor.

As that man went down, a whiskey bottle thrown by Albert flew from behind the bar and nailed another hombre in the back of the head.

The bottle was heavy glass, and it didn't break. The man's head didn't break, either, but it must have cracked. His hat flew off, his eyes bugged out, and he sprawled across a table and lay still.

That left three gunmen. Angelique shoved the table into the man opposite her and then turned the table over on him. Fargo saw his legs kicking as he tried to get free. One arm stuck out from under the table, and his fingers scrabbled for his pistol, which lay a foot or so away. To be sure he didn't reach it, Fargo shot him in the hand.

The man whinnied like a kicked horse, and Angelique snatched up the pistol. She held it in both hands and fired it at the table. Wood chunks flew up as the bullets smashed through the bottom of the table.

Hawkins rolled off the piano bench and grabbed a chair. He hit the man closest to him across the body, shattering the chair and knocking the man to the side. The man turned to shoot Hawkins, but Hawkins hit him again. This time one of the chair legs caught his fore-head, and he stumbled to his left, fell over another chair, and hit the floor.

That left one man. Or it would have left one if he'd still been around. There was no sign of him.

Gun smoke filled the air and Fargo's nostrils. He waved a hand in front of his face and looked around, but he still couldn't see the fifth man.

"Upstairs," Albert said.

"Get him," Angelique said.

She still held the pistol, and Fargo figured it had a couple of bullets left in case either of the unconscious men wanted to try anything. Which seemed unlikely.

Fargo nodded to Angelique and went up the stairs.

When he reached the head of the stairs, Fargo saw only one room had an open door. It wasn't Angelique's room.

Fargo heard the sound of struggling in the room. He took a step down the hall, and the man came out of the room, holding Rose in front of him.

Rose twisted and kicked backwards at the man's legs, but the man had his left arm clamped around her neck, cutting off her air, and she didn't kick long. Her face got red as she clawed at the arm, trying to move it. The man held fast and jerked her head back.

Rose opened her mouth to scream, but no sound came out.

"I'm leaving now," the man said. He laid his pistol alongside Rose's head. "You try to stop me, I'll kill her. Lay your gun on the floor, you son of a bitch."

A woman stuck her head out of a door down the hall.

"Get back in there, or I'll shoot," the man said without turning around. The woman ducked back inside.

Fargo laid the pistol down on the floor.

"Step aside and let those people downstairs know I'm comin'," the man said. "Tell 'em if they mess with me, this bitch is dead."

Fargo moved against the wall and called down the stairs. "Man's coming down with Rose. Don't try to stop him."

When the man reached Fargo, he kicked the .44 in front of him. It flew straight out and hit the step next to the bottom of the stairway. It bounced off and landed on the floor.

"Now you move on up past me," the man said to Fargo. "Put your hands in your pants and slide along the wall." He tapped the side of Rose's head with his pistol. "You make a grab at me, I'll shoot the top of her head off."

Fargo did as he was told. The man and Rose passed him and started down the stairs. Fargo let him get by, then reached down and slipped the Arkansas toothpick from its sheath low on his leg.

The man was halfway down the stairs. He was having trouble negotiating them with Rose, though she'd stopped struggling. Fargo wasn't sure she was even still alive, but she was. She had enough fight left in her to make one halfhearted kick.

It was enough to throw the man off balance. His foot missed the next step, and he and Rose tumbled the rest of the way down the stairs together.

They hit the floor in a heap, and the man pushed himself away from her.

Fargo heard a pistol blast as Angelique cut loose. Two bullets ripped the planks of the wall near the man as he got to his feet.

He brought up his pistol, ready to kill Angelique, not worried about Fargo at the moment. He should have been, however, because the Trailsman sent the Arkansas toothpick pinwheeling down the stairs. Its point hit the man's gun arm and went right on through, striking a rib before it stopped.

That pretty much put an end to the man's ambition to shoot Angelique. His pistol dropped from his fingers, and he stepped back to the wall, resting his back against it before sliding down to sit on the floor, his mouth open and twisted, his left hand yanking at the handle of the big knife.

Fargo clattered down the stairs and stood above him. "Let me get that for you," he said.

Fargo reached down and took hold of his knife by the handle. He gave an abrupt yank and pulled it out of the man's arm. He wiped off the blood and slipped the knife back in its sheath. Then he picked up his pistol and holstered it. He noticed that Angelique was no longer holding the gun she'd picked up. It lay on the floor by the table where it had first fallen.

Blood soaked the sleeve of the man's shirt and dripped on the floor.

"God's sake," he said. "Help me."

"Glad to," Fargo said. "First, though, we need to see about Rose."

Rose lay on the floor beside the man. She gasped for breath. Angelique came over, and she and Fargo got Rose into a chair.

"She'll be all right," Angelique said. "Albert, bring a glass of brandy. Bring one for Sam, too."

The piano player had risen from the floor and was seated by Rose.

Albert came over with a couple of glasses. Angelique took one from him and gave Rose a sip. Hawkins took the other and downed a healthy slug of brandy.

"That was quite a throw you made," Fargo told Albert.

"Used to hunt rabbits with rocks when I was a kid," Albert said. "Didn't have the money for bullets. I got to where I could throw pretty good."

"Shit, who cares?" said the man on the floor. "Get me some help."

"We'll see about that," Fargo said. "You and me need to do some talking."

"Talking about what? What the hell's goin' on here?" Marshal Tatum shouted as he pushed through the batwing doors. He held his pistol in his hand. "From where I was, it sounded like a damn war."

"These men tried to kill us," Angelique said. "They didn't manage it, though." She gestured to Rose, who sat sipping the brandy. "They almost got Rose."

Tatum looked around the room. "Looks like you're all still alive, all right. How many of 'em did you kill?"

"Don't know," Fargo said. "Haven't had time to see. I figure Corby Carson's gonna have himself some more business, though."

"Damn right, he is." Tatum holstered his pistol and went around the room looking at the downed men. "Two of 'em will be all right, I guess, and that one you got bleedin' on the floor there oughta live. Help him get up, Fargo."

Fargo gripped the man's good arm and heaved. The man stood up, clutching his bad arm.

"I gotta have a doctor," he whined.

"We'll see about that," Tatum told him. He nudged the man Albert's bottle had struck. The man didn't move. "Looks like this 'un needs a doctor, too. Albert, you and Hawkins get hold of him and take him to the jail."

Hawkins finished off his brandy and joined Albert at the fallen man. While he and the bartender were following Tatum's orders, the man Hawkins had hit with the chair sat up and looked around. Tatum pulled him to his feet.

"You come on with me," he said. "Fargo, you bring that one you got."

Without waiting for a response, Tatum dragged his man stumbling across the floor and went through the batwings. Fargo noticed that a crowd had gathered outside. Likely most of them wouldn't be coming in for a drink.

"What do you think, Miss Leblanc?" Albert said.

He had hold of the unconscious man's ankles. Hawkins had him by the shoulders.

"You'd better do as he said," Angelique said. "You, too, Skye. Maybe he'll talk to you on the way."

Fargo didn't think so. He wasn't happy with the way things had turned out, but there wasn't anything he could do about it now. He gave the man's arm a pull and said, "Come on."

The man winced. "You're hurtin' me."

"I'll hurt you a hell of a lot worse if you don't come on," Fargo told him.

He didn't give Fargo any trouble after that. They went out the door and through the buzzing crowd.

The man wouldn't say a word as they walked to the jail. When they arrived, Tatum locked the man in a cell with his two friends. Albert and Hawkins were already gone.

"I sent Hawkins for Corby Carson, and Albert went for the doctor," Tatum said when Fargo asked. "Can't just let these men die."

"They'll die anyway after they're tried," Fargo said. "Bound to hang for trying to kill everybody in the saloon."

"Maybe so, but they won't die before their time comes, not in my jail, they won't. And since they didn't kill anybody, they might not get hung. They might get sent to the pen at Little Rock."

From what Fargo had heard of the penitentiary, the men might have preferred hanging.

"I need to talk to them," he said. "Find out who sent them to the saloon."

"Nope. Can't let you do that, Fargo. You can talk to 'em after the doc gets 'em fixed up, but until then, they don't talk to anybody."

"You making any progress toward finding out who killed Harragan's son?" Fargo said.

"What brought that up?"

"Might have been one of those fellas in the cells. You need to find out if it was, and you need to find out who they're working for."

"I don't need you to tell me my business," Tatum said. "I'll question them when the doctor's done with 'em."

"You'll tell me what you find out if I come by, I guess."

"If I think it's any of your business. Right now, I'm not so sure it is."

"I think it is," Fargo said.

Tatum gave him a gap-toothed grin. "And I don't care what you think. I'm the marshal, and you're just a hired gun who's killed . . . what? Two more men today? You've killed so many I'm losin' count, Fargo, and that's not good."

Fargo didn't like being called a hired gun, but he figured that's what he was for the time being, even if it wasn't by choice. He didn't bother to tell Tatum that one of the dead men in the saloon had been shot by Angelique.

"There was another man," Fargo said. "Not that I killed. He doesn't have a scratch on him. He was in the saloon, but he ran for it when the shooting started. He's on the loose somewhere."

117

"I wouldn't worry about him, then," Tatum said. "He's probably halfway to Texas by now."

Fargo didn't think so, but he didn't argue.

"You got anything else to say?" Tatum asked.

"Guess not," Fargo said.

"Then you better go back to the Traveler and help Corby with the bodies. You oughta be gettin' good at that by now."

Fargo didn't reply. He touched a finger to the brim of his hat and got out of there.

10

Both Hawkins and Albert were back at the Traveler when Fargo arrived. Albert was mopping some of the blood off the floor, and Hawkins was sitting at the piano looking bemused. The two bodies still lay where they'd fallen.

"Where's Angelique?" Fargo said.

"Upstairs with Rose and the rest of the girls," Hawkins said. The toothpick between his lips jumped a little. Even with all that ruckus going on, he hadn't lost it. "They needed a little calming down."

Fargo heard a wagon creak and rattle outside, and after a short interval Corby Carson came inside.

"Damnation, Fargo," he said, giving the room the once-over. "You're a regular one-man army if there ever was one. I oughta make you a partner in my business."

"I'll pass," Fargo said.

"I didn't offer. Just said I oughta. You gonna help me get these two dead fellas out of here?"

"Sure," Fargo said. "Least I can do for a partner."

"You ain't my partner. I was joshin'. I wouldn't want you around. Liable to be too dangerous for me. I'd just as soon you'd slow down on the killin', too, to tell you the truth. I'm tired of all this work."

"I'm tired of the killing, too," Fargo said. "Let's get these bodies loaded on your wagon."

After the job was done and Carson had left, Fargo went back in the Traveler. Albert had the floor just about clean, and Hawkins was setting the tables aright.

"I'm going to the Grand Hotel to see Harragan," Fargo said. "I'll be back later."

"You don't have to worry about us," Albert told him. "I figure business will be mighty slow today."

Fargo thought Albert was right. He went back outside, but nobody was looking to come to the Traveler. While he watched, a couple of men even walked across the street to avoid the place.

Fargo shrugged and started toward the Grand. People looked at him sideways as he passed. He was getting quite a reputation in Hot Springs, and it wasn't one he appreciated.

When Fargo reached the hotel a few minutes later, this time Harragan was eager to see him.

"I heard about the trouble at the Traveler," Harragan said. He passed a hand over his eye patch as if checking for the missing eye. "You know Brundage is behind it."

"Convince me," Fargo said.

"You saw what he did yesterday. The man's heartless. He's out to ruin Miss Leblanc, and me, too."

"You had any trouble lately?"

"No, but it's coming. You can bet on that."

They were in Harragan's office, Harragan behind his desk and Fargo in one of the big oak chairs.

"Tatum will take care of you," Fargo said.

"I can't count on that. Sure, he comes here now and then to get his payoff. You didn't know about that, did you. I pay him to give me a little extra protection, and so far it's worked out to my advantage. He hasn't found out anything about who killed my son, though."

Fargo wondered why Angelique hadn't thought of the protection angle, but he didn't pursue that line of conversation. He said, "How much do you know about Brundage?"

"What do you mean?"

"I mean where did he come from?"

"Back east, that's all I know."

"Why would he come here?"

"Don't ask me. I'm not friendly with him."

"What about his sister?"

Harragan sat up straight. "What's that supposed to mean?"

"Nothing," Fargo said. "I just wondered if she was as good a churchgoer as her brother."

"I'm not much on church, myself, so I wouldn't know about that." Harragan gave Fargo a speculative look. "You sure you don't want to go to work for me? Between the two of us, we could get rid of Brundage. Then Miss Leblanc wouldn't have to worry anymore."

"I'll think about it," Fargo said.

Fargo's next stop was the Superior Hotel. Brundage was indisposed, but Prudence was happy to see him.

"Come along to my room," she said. "We can talk there."

Fargo could see from the look in her eyes that she had more in mind than talking. That was all right as far as he was concerned, though he wondered if what she wanted from him was more than a good time.

A good time was all she seemed to care about, however. As soon as they were in her room, she locked the door and began to kiss him. Soon their clothes were off, and they stood facing each other only inches apart.

Fargo admired the shape of her firm breasts, the smooth length of her thighs, the flat curve of her belly, and more.

"You like what you see?" Prudence said.

Fargo nodded, his throat dry.

"So do I," she said, and she reached for his erect manhood. She clasped it in her hand. "I like what I feel, too."

Fargo cupped her firm breasts, teasing the nipples with his thumbs. "Do you like the way that feels?"

"Ummm," she said. "I do, I truly do." She began to massage his stiff rod. "How about you?"

"Yes," Fargo said.

Keeping him firmly in hand, she led him to the bed. Then she released him and lay down on her back, her hair spread on the pillow, her legs wantonly apart.

"What do you see now, Fargo? Something you like?"

"I like everything I see," he said.

"Then stop looking and prove it to me."

Fargo sank to his knees beside the bed and kissed the curve of Prudence's belly. She sighed and pushed gently on the top of his head, so he moved down farther, getting right to the heart of the matter.

Prudence shuddered. "Oh, yes, yes. That's right, Fargo, that's right."

She put her hands behind his head and pulled him to her. As she did, he bit down gently on her fleshy mound. She moaned so loudly that Fargo thought she might have been heard, but no one came to interrupt them. His tongue worked her slit, and soon she was quivering with delight, her breath coming faster and faster.

"Don't stop, Fargo," she said, twining her fingers in his hair. "Don't stop."

He didn't stop, not until she reached a terrific climax. She arched her back and bucked like a young bronc, repeating his name over and over, then suddenly relaxed and fell silent.

Fargo didn't give her any time to rest. He raised himself off the floor and hovered over her.

Prudence looked into his eyes. "You know what I want, Fargo. Let me have it."

Fargo didn't need any further encouragement. He sank his shaft into her as far as it would go. She gripped him with her legs and held him there, grinding herself against him for a moment. When she released him, he began pumping, slowly at first and then faster and faster. She matched his every movement with one of her own, and soon he knew that both of them were at the point of no return. He let himself go and released a scalding torrent that seemed to go on and on while she whipped her head back and forth, her hair slapping across his face.

When it was finally over, they lay side by side. Prudence said, "Fargo, how did you get to know Angelique?"

"I've known her for a long time," he said.

"Since before she came to Hot Springs?"

"That's right."

"You knew her in Saint Louis?"

"Yes, and I knew what she did there."

"It doesn't bother you?"

"Not a bit," Fargo said. "It bothers your brother, though."

"He's a churchgoing man. He believes women should be pure."

Fargo didn't know what to say to that, so he kept quiet.

"I'm not exactly pure," Prudence said. "You might have noticed that."

"I'm not your brother."

Prudence laughed. "You're certainly not, and it's a good thing, too."

"I mean I'm not judging you. I'm not in any position to do that."

"I like your position," Prudence said. "I liked it even more a little while ago."

Fargo wondered where the conversation was going. Prudence was quiet for a moment. Then she went on. "It's not my fault that Clyde found out about your friend Angelique."

"I never said it was."

"But I knew her in Saint Louis."

"I see," Fargo said, though he didn't, not really. However, he was getting an idea.

"I worked there," Prudence said. "Just like Angelique did. She never knew me, but I saw her a few times."

"And you told your brother."

"No. That's the strange thing. I never did."

Prudence sat up. Fargo looked at her breasts, and she said, "Pay attention now."

"I am," Fargo said.

"To what I'm saying."

"Oh."

"Clyde and I grew up in a strict family. Clyde's like our parents. I'm not."

Fargo grinned. "I kind of figured that out for myself."

"I ran away," Prudence said. "I loved them, but I couldn't live like them. I wanted something different from my life. For a while I had that."

Fargo could understand the urge to break free of restrictions. He would never have been able to live what most people considered a normal life, trapped in a city, doing a regular job.

"Clyde found out where I was," Prudence went on. "It took him a while, but when he did, he came after me. He said we could never go back home because I'd shamed the family but that he knew a place where we could make a new start. Our parents had money, and they gave Clyde enough to come here and buy this hotel. Now it looks like we might not have it long."

"Why's that?"

"Steve Harragan's trying to take it away from us. He knows Clyde will never sell, so that's why he's causing us so much trouble. He's the one who's out to ruin your friend Angelique, too."

Fargo kept hearing the same story from both sides, and he didn't know who to believe. He figured about the only way he could find out the truth was if one of the men in Tatum's jail talked.

"Harragan says the same about you and Clyde," Fargo told her. "That you're trying to ruin him."

"You can't believe that, not after . . . not now."

Maybe that was it, Fargo thought. Maybe Prudence's interest in him wasn't purely the pleasure she took from their bedroom exertions. She might have been trying to win him over to the belief that she and Clyde were innocent of doing anything to destroy Harragan and Angelique, but he didn't think so.

"Harragan's the one who told Clyde about Angelique," Prudence said. "Not me. Can't you see that?"

Fargo had a hard time with it. How could Harragan have known about Angelique? According to David, he'd never left the farm before coming down to Hot Springs.

It was all too much for Fargo. He needed to leave and clear his head. He got off the bed.

"You don't believe me, do you?" Prudence asked.

"Yeah, I do," Fargo said, keeping his tone neutral.

"I'm telling the truth. What are you going to do about it?"

"I don't know," Fargo replied honestly.

"You'd better do something before Harragan gets rid of all of us."

"That much I do know," Fargo said.

"You understand why Clyde's the way he is?"

"You mean why he accepts you and not Angelique?"

"Yes. He hates what I did, but I'm his sister, not his wife. You see?"

"Not really," Fargo said. He felt that way about a lot of the things he'd run into since arriving in Hot Springs.

Prudence didn't try to persuade Fargo to stay, and in fact she didn't seem sorry to see him go. He got dressed and left the hotel without talking to Brundage. It seemed like a good idea to get away from town for a while, get out into the hills and trees where he could think things over.

But he didn't get the chance. He'd barely cleared the doorway of the hotel when he heard gunshots and saw people near the jail ducking for cover.

"Damnation," Fargo said, and he started to run.

Before he reached the jail, he saw a man dash out the door. He stopped in the street, turned, and fired his pistol back into the building.

Fargo knew the man. He was the one who'd run from the saloon before the fighting got too bloody. This time he wasn't going to get away so easily. Someone inside the jail returned his fire, and he crumpled in the street.

Fargo stopped running. He could tell from the way the man had fallen that he wouldn't be getting up again. Fargo had a feeling that there were other dead men inside the jail, too, and he was right.

Hank Tatum came outside. He was so tall he nearly had to duck to come through the door. He held a pistol in his right hand, smoke coming from the barrel.

Tatum looked up and down the street as if wondering where the man had gone. When he saw Fargo, he said, "Watch yourself, Fargo. There might be more of 'em."

There weren't any more of them, however, and Fargo knew it.

"You got the last one," he said. He'd reached the man in the street, so he bent down and took the pistol from his hand just in case. "What about your prisoners?"

"Dead, I expect," Tatum said.

"All three of them?"

"All three. The doctor'd just left after gettin' 'em bandaged up when that fella there came in." He indicated the dead man with a quick flick of his pistol barrel. "Said he was a friend of theirs and wanted to talk to 'em. I said he couldn't do that. Next thing I knew, he'd whipped out his gun and started shootin' into the cell block through the open door. By the time I got my own gun out, he was on the run."

"He didn't run far," the Trailsman said.

"And it's a good thing, too. No tellin' who else he might've killed. He was sure as hell tryin' to kill me."

"Yeah," Fargo said. "I can see that."

"Won't have to hold a trial now," Tatum said. "Those men probably would've been hung, anyway."

"Or sent to the pen."

"Yeah, well, they don't have to worry about that now."

"And neither do you," Fargo said.

"You got some kind of problem with what happened here?" Tatum snapped.

"Nope. I can see what happened. Self-defense. I guess you didn't get a chance to question any of them before they were killed."

"Hell, no. Like I told you, the doc just got finished with 'em before they were shot. Bastard shot 'em in the cell like trapped animals. I didn't even get to ask their names."

"Too bad," Fargo said. "Well, this time it's you that gets to help Carson load up his wagon."

"Four more dead," Tatum said. "If you stay around here much longer, Fargo, there's not gonna be anybody left alive."

"There'll be me," Fargo said.

*　　*　　*

Outside of town, but not so far that the hotels weren't still visible through the trees, there was a small spring in a grove of pines. The spring wasn't big enough to make anyone want to build a hotel nearby, but it was just fine if two people wanted to sit quietly and talk.

And that was what Fargo wanted to do. He'd gone back to the hotel, explained to Angelique what had happened, and asked her to take a walk with him to somewhere peaceful. She was the one who'd suggested the spring.

"What do you think about it all, Skye?" she said.

"I think somebody's lying to me," he said.

"Not me, I hope."

A few rusty-colored pine needles drifted down and landed in the spring. Fargo watched them float there for a second or two.

"No, not you," he said. "It's either Harragan or Brundage." Fargo didn't think it would be wise to specify which Brundage he meant. "One of them's causing the problems for you. Those men in the jail knew who was behind it, but they won't be telling now."

"None of them were from around here."

"No, they were brought in from somewhere else."

Angelique thought that over. "Clyde never goes anywhere," she said after a while. "Harragan's the one who leaves town on business now and then."

"There's a telegraph office. Brundage could hire people easily enough."

"If he knew them. He's not from around here. How would he know anybody?"

She had a point, though Fargo was pretty sure Brundage could find the men he needed without much trouble. Prudence probably knew a few from her days in Saint Louis. A farmer like Harragan wasn't likely to know anyone, any more than Brundage was.

Unless . . .

Unless Harragan wasn't really Harragan. If that was the case, then a lot of things would make sense.

Fargo stood up. He'd known from the beginning that something wasn't right, but he hadn't been able to pin anything down. Now everything that had bothered him seemed to line up in his head.

"What's the matter?" Angelique said.

"What if Harragan isn't who he says he is?"

Angelique gave him a puzzled look. "What do you mean?"

"I mean what if Harragan isn't Harragan? What if he's somebody else?"

"I don't understand. Of course he's Harragan."

"Maybe not," Fargo said. "Dave Harragan never called his pa anything but Steven. Everybody here calls him Steve."

Angelique laughed. "That's a pretty weak argument."

Fargo admitted that she was right. "But that's not all. Harragan was a farmer. He didn't have any money. How did he buy the hotel?"

"He won the money playing cards," Angelique said. "He just got lucky."

"No, he didn't," Fargo said. "I talked to the gamblers in the Traveler. They didn't remember Harragan as a winner. They said he wasn't even a very good cardplayer."

Angelique reached up to take Fargo's hand. She gave a tug, and he sank back down beside here.

"He could have gotten the money somewhere else," Angelique suggested.

"Where? A farmer doesn't make that kind of money, not on the kind of little place Harragan had. Not even on a bigger one."

Angelique didn't have an answer for that, and Fargo

tried to remember everything he'd heard about what had happened around the time Harragan arrived in Hot Springs.

"The Overland Mail," Fargo said after a while. "When was that big robbery?"

That got Angelique's attention. "It wasn't long after they started coming through Hot Springs. About a year and a half ago. They never did catch the robbers."

"And when did Harragan get to town?"

"It wasn't long after that," Angelique said. "But Harragan said he came from some farm to heal up his leg."

"Healed up mighty quick, didn't it? And he doesn't even have much of a limp anymore."

"That's right," Angelique said. "That's what the waters here are supposed to do. That's why people come. Besides, what about his eye?"

"Anybody can wear a patch," Fargo said. "Doesn't mean he's lost an eye. We don't know that Harragan has, either."

"If you're right," Angelique said, "then Harragan, or whoever he is, left town before his son, or Harragan's son . . . This is confusing me."

"Just call him Harragan. That's what he's calling himself now. He left town because he didn't want to be here in case Dave got by the killers he'd sent for him."

"But Dave did get by them, thanks to you."

"Harragan had something in mind for him if that happened. A room ready at the hotel, and you can bet somebody knew which room it was."

"Who?"

"My guess is Tatum. According to Carson, he came here about the same time Harragan did. Harragan set himself up as a hotel owner and helped get Tatum appointed town marshal. I'd bet Tatum was in on the robbery, too."

It fit together just fine, Fargo thought. Tatum was easily big enough to have killed Dave with a blow to the head and carried him down to the spring. Dave would have been happy to let the town marshal in his room, and Tatum could have done him in right there. Even if the blow hadn't killed him, Tatum could have knocked him unconscious, taken him down to the spring, and held him under until he drowned.

The robbery explained the bare walls in the jail. No wonder Tatum didn't have any wanted flyers. He wouldn't want to slip up and have somebody see one of him or Harragan.

And no wonder he never seemed to arrive at the Traveler in time to be of any help, or that he met with Harragan every week. It wasn't for a payoff. The two of them were setting things up for their eventual takeover of the whole town. If things went like they planned, they'd own two hotels and the best saloon in Hot Springs.

That might have been just the start, but it was a good one. Soon they'd move on to other properties. Harragan would arrange for a few minor incidents at his place to make it look as if he were being attacked, too. He'd even started the fight with Brundage at the cemetery as part of his cover.

Harragan must have met Angelique in Saint Louis or known about her. She wouldn't necessarily have remembered him. He'd told Brundage about her so the two of them wouldn't get together to buck him as he tried to take over their establishments.

It was a good plan, and it might have worked, but Fargo was going to see to it that it didn't pan out.

"You can't prove any of that," Angelique said when Fargo laid it out for her.

"Nope. Sure can't. But it's the way of it, or pretty close. It's the only thing that makes sense."

"But how could Harragan—*this* Harragan, I mean—how could he have found out about the other one? And what happened to the other one?"

"I'd bet they met on the trail not long after that robbery. The real Harragan didn't have any idea who the owlhoot was. They must have talked, and Dave's pa told his story. The owlhoot killed him and took his name and his eye patch and showed up here."

"I think I see it now," Angelique said. "He had a new name and a perfect way to spend his money, or some of it. If he claimed he won it gambling, nobody would think a hotel owner would be a stage robber. He could spend the rest of his life here and never get caught."

"That's about it, and he would've been fine if he hadn't gotten greedy. He's not going to let anybody stop him from taking your place and Brundage's if he can help it. He had those men killed today so they couldn't talk, and Tatum killed the last one of them. Nobody's left to tie Harragan to anything."

Something else occurred to Fargo as he was talking. How had the gunman who'd been waiting for him in the saloon known he'd be coming in through the back door? Tatum must have told the men that Fargo was on his way to the saloon. He was the only one who could have. No wonder he'd left the jail in such a hurry. After he warned them, the men had been prepared for anything Fargo might do.

"They're ruthless," Angelique said.

"They sure enough are. The thing now is to figure out what we're gonna do about them."

"What can we do? Tatum's the law, and Harragan might have other men lined up to gun you down if he realizes you know what's going on."

"We'll figure something out," Fargo said. "Let's go back to town."

He stood up and took Angelique's hand, pulling her to her feet.

"I'm lucky he didn't have me killed," Angelique said.

"He had something else in mind for you," Fargo said, "and he wasn't ready to start killing people. Then I came to town. He's had to change his plans."

"What do you think he'll do now?"

"He doesn't know we're onto him. We'll just have to be careful."

"Somehow I don't think of you as a careful man," Angelique said.

Fargo grinned. "I'll just have to change my ways, then."

"See that you do. I can't afford to lose you, not now. Not ever."

"I'll be careful," Fargo said, and he almost believed it.

11

The afternoon went by quietly. Fargo sat in the saloon and listened to the piano tinkling away. He watched the drinkers and the gamblers. There was no sign of trouble, and Fargo wondered if Harragan had used up his supply of hired guns. It was possible, even likely.

That wasn't necessarily a good thing, however. If Harragan thought he was being pushed to the wall, he might try something desperate.

Fargo didn't know what that might be, but he could think of a couple of things. The most likely would be some attempt to get Fargo out of the way. Tatum was right about the number of bodies that had piled up since Fargo had gotten into town, not that it was Fargo's fault. Still, Harragan couldn't be happy with the way things had turned out. Get rid of Fargo, though, and he could bring in some more men and go right back to working on his plan.

Maybe that would be the way of it. Harragan had been patient up until now, and he might not see any need to change. If so, Fargo would have to be careful that he didn't wind up with a back full of lead.

While he was sitting quietly and thinking those pleasant thoughts, Marshal Tatum showed up. He stood in the doorway, blocking most of the light.

"I need to talk to you, Fargo," he said.

"Come on in," Fargo said. He didn't get up. He pushed a chair away from the table with one foot. "Bring the marshal a drink, Albert."

"I don't want a drink, and I'm not coming in," Tatum said. "You need to come with me."

Fargo didn't like the sound of that one bit. "I don't think so. I'm enjoying listening to Sam play the piano, and I was about to have a whiskey. You can join me."

Tatum pulled his pistol. "You're gonna join me, Fargo, like I said. Now get up and come along."

Fargo thought it over. He might have a chance if he went for his gun, but as Angelique had said, Tatum was the law. Harragan would make a stink if Fargo shot him. Fargo might even end up in jail.

Even worse, though Fargo didn't think it would happen, Tatum might shoot him, even kill him. Better to go on to the jail and see what developed.

Fargo stood up and spread his hands. "All right, Tatum. I'll come with you. You want to tell me why?"

"I'll tell you later."

"Don't go, Skye," Angelique said. She had been in her room, but now she stood at the head of the stairs. "Stay here. He can't make you go anywhere unless he arrests you."

"I didn't want to have to do that," Tatum said, "but I will if I have to."

"I'll be all right," Fargo told Angelique. "You'll know where I am." He looked around the saloon. "Everybody will know, Tatum."

"Fine with me," Tatum said. "You comin', or do I have to come and get you?"

"I'm coming."

Fargo walked across the saloon. As soon as he got to Tatum, the marshal grabbed hold of Fargo's right arm, twisted it behind his back, and spun Fargo around. He stuck his pistol barrel against the base of Fargo's skull.

If he hadn't been surprised yet again, Fargo might have been able to put up a fight. Tatum was bigger, but Fargo figured it would have been an even fight. As it was, Tatum had him trapped.

"I'm arresting you now, Fargo," Tatum said.

"What for?" Angelique yelled. "Tell us, damn you!"

"Robbery," Tatum said. "This is the man who robbed the Overland Stage."

As Tatum pulled Fargo out the door, the Trailsman tried to count up the number of surprises he'd had in Hot Springs, but by now he couldn't even remember all of them. It wasn't a good feeling.

He should have considered the possibility that Harragan would be tired having his plans thwarted and would do something to get rid of Fargo. Even if he'd thought of it, though, Fargo would never have guessed that Harragan would have him arrested for the very robbery that he'd committed himself.

"Planning to shoot me when I try to escape?" Fargo asked Tatum when the got to the street.

"Could be," Tatum said. He whacked the Trailsman lightly on the side of the head with his pistol barrel. "I'd be glad to if you'd give me a good reason. You gonna try to run?"

The town had already had quite a show that day, what with the shootings at the jail, and the few people out on the street in the late afternoon watched as if expecting more violence. Fargo wasn't sorry to disappoint them.

"Not me," Fargo said. "I'm just doing what you say."

"Hey!" came a shout from behind them.

Fargo turned his head to see who it was. Tatum whacked him with the pistol again, and Fargo told himself he'd make the marshal pay for that.

Albert and Sam trotted into the street and caught up with Fargo and Tatum.

"Angelique sent us along to sit with Fargo while he's in jail," Sam said. "Just to be sure he's all right."

"You can't do that," Tatum told them.

"Bullshit," Albert said. "It's the town's jail. We can sit in it if we want to."

"Angelique's gonna bring us supper from the boardinghouse," Sam said. "We can stay there as long as we need to."

Fargo grinned. It looked like he wasn't going to get shot while escaping, at least not right then.

"Damn it," Tatum said.

"Too bad I couldn't bring the piano along," Sam said. "Ain't nothing like a little music to pass the time."

Tatum gave Fargo a rough jerk. "Come on, Fargo. You're gonna get locked up tight, and if these two want to watch, they're welcome."

He didn't sound like he meant it. Fargo hoped Tatum wouldn't organize a jailbreak to be conducted by more of Harragan's men. He knew he'd never survive if that happened. Neither would Sam and Albert.

When they got to the jail, Tatum took Fargo's gun and knife and locked them in a desk drawer. He locked Fargo in a cell that was still spattered with the dried blood of the previous occupants. Tatum put the key to the cell in his pocket and turned to Albert and Sam.

"I have to go out for a little while. Get me some supper, do a little law business. You two can stay here if you want to. You can even feed Fargo if somebody brings something. I'll be back."

"You trust us not to break him out?" Albert said.

Tatum laughed. "You couldn't do it if you wanted to. Those walls are solid rock, the bars are steel, and I got the key." He patted his pocket.

"I guess we won't even try, then," Albert said.

"Wouldn't do you any good," Tatum said, and left them there.

When he was gone, Sam said, "You reckon he's gonna send somebody here to kill us all, Fargo?"

Fargo took off his hat and sat on the rickety cot in the cell. The mattress was as thin as folding money.

"Not yet, but it might be a good idea if you went on back to the saloon. Tell Angelique I'll be fine."

"Yeah," Sam said, "except you won't. You need to get out of here before Tatum comes back."

"How's he gonna do that?" Albert said.

"I don't know," Sam said.

Fargo lay back on the cot and stared at the ceiling.

"You gonna take a nap?" Albert said.

"It's a little late for that," Sam said. "It's already gettin' dark. Be time to bed down for the night in a little while."

Fargo sat up. "Tell you what. You go back to the saloon and tell Angelique to have Corby Carson bring his wagon over to the alley in back of this place quick as he can. Have him bring his coffin-making tools, too."

"You gonna get measured for a casket, Fargo?" Sam said.

"Be a good idea, considering where I am," Fargo said. "You go on and do what I asked you to."

"Angelique won't like it."

"Tell her to come on over and talk to me about it," Fargo said.

"What do you think, Albert?" Sam said.

"Hell, I get paid to pour drinks, not think. Let's go see Angelique."

Fargo heard the wagon before Carson got to the jail. It was a good thing Tatum wasn't back yet.

"He's making plenty of noise," Angelique said. She was standing outside the cell. "Do you think we have time for this?"

"I hope so," Fargo said. "Go on back there and tell him what do to. Get a pry bar while you're at it and see if you can get my gun and knife."

Angelique had already tried the locked drawer, without success. She left, and Fargo looked up at the tiny slit in the wall that served as a window. It wasn't full dark, but it was dark enough for what he had planned.

He heard Carson and Angelique talking quietly. Then Carson's voice got loud.

"I'm an old man. I can't do that."

"Yes, you can," Angelique said. "Put that toolbox on the wagon seat and stand on it."

"I'll fall."

"No, you won't. You get up there and punch a hole in that roof."

Carson argued some more, but Fargo knew he'd give in. Hardly anybody ever won an argument with Angelique. Sooner or later Carson would climb up on the roof, which was the cell's weakness. The walls were stone, the bars were steel, but the roof was made of wood.

It wasn't long before Fargo heard boots scrabbling against the wall as Carson pulled himself up on the roof.

"Gimme that hand ax," he said.

"Here," Angelique said.

Footsteps above him let Fargo know that Carson was moving on the roof. When the footsteps ended, the ax thunked into the shingles above Fargo's head. The noise was loud, and Fargo hoped it didn't disturb anybody who happened to pass in the street. The good thing about it was that it would cover the noise of Angelique working on the desk drawer.

He could hear her in the office. In a few minutes he

heard the drawer splinter, and Angelique came in with his .44 and the Arkansas toothpick. Fargo felt better with them back where they belonged, even if he was still in the cell.

Before long, wood chips rained down on Fargo's head. He told Angelique to go back to the alley, and soon after that, Carson had opened a good-sized hole.

"You in there, Fargo?" he said.

"I am," Fargo said. "But not for long."

He stood on the cot, grabbed the edge of the hole, and pulled himself up and through it.

"Damn," Carson said. "You sure got up here easier than I did."

"Let's talk about it after we get down," Fargo said.

He went to the edge of the roof and dropped into the wagon. Reaching up, he took the hand ax from Carson and put it in the toolbox.

"Give me a little help here," Carson said. He was sitting with his legs dangling over the alley. "Elsewise, I'm gonna have to jump and break my fool neck."

Fargo reached up, took Carson's arms, and swung him down.

"Where to now?" Angelique said.

"The Grand," Fargo said. "That's where Tatum must be."

"What're you gonna do if he is?" Carson said.

"I'll worry about that later. Just drive us around to the back of the hotel."

"You gonna pay me for all this trouble?"

"Think of all the business I already brought you. The way I see it, you owe me."

"Damn," Carson said. "You got a point there."

"We'll just lie in the wagon bed," Fargo said. "We don't want anybody to see us. Stay in the alleys as much as you can."

Carson didn't answer. He clucked to his horse and twitched the reins. The wagon moved, and Fargo and Angelique lay down in the bed.

"This would be a good time to tell me you have a plan," Angelique said, pillowing her head on Fargo's shoulder.

"I wish I could tell you I had one, but you heard what I said to Carson."

"I thought you were joking."

"Not a chance," Fargo said with a grim little smile.

The wagon came to a stop a few moments later. Fargo sat up and looked around. He saw the long wall of the hotel and several lighted windows, but he didn't see what he was looking for.

"There's supposed to be a back door to Harragan's office," he said, keeping his voice down.

"Ain't my fault if you can't find it," Carson said from his place on the wagon seat. "You said bring you, so I brung you. Ain't my fault if you can't find the door. What you do now is up to you."

Fargo slipped over the side of the wagon. "I appreciate your help. You take Miss Leblanc back to the Traveler, now, and then you can get on back to your place."

"I'm staying with you," Angelique said.

She was dressed for the job in denim pants, boots, and a man's shirt. She dropped to the ground beside Fargo.

Fargo opened his mouth, then shut it. Nothing he said would do any good. What he'd said about nobody winning an argument with Angelique went for him, too.

"So long, then," Carson said.

He flicked the reins and the wagon moved away.

"Let's find that door," Fargo said.

It didn't take them long, even in the dark. A step made out of a pine stump stood against the wall, and there was the door. The trouble was that it didn't have a handle.

"It must open only from the inside," Fargo said. "People who come to see Harragan have to knock before he lets them in."

"Not a bad idea," Angelique said. "That way he knows who he's letting in. I don't think you'd have a chance. But I might."

"That's not a good idea," Fargo said. "You're not even supposed to know about this door."

"Half the town knows about it. Besides, it makes sense for me to be here and come in through the back if I wanted to talk to him about what Tatum's done with you."

Fargo thought about that. It made sense, all right, and Harragan just might be fooled. It was about time somebody surprised him.

"All right," Fargo said. "You knock, and if Harragan says he's going to let you in, stand aside."

Angelique stepped up on the stump and rapped on the door with her knuckles. At first there was no response, and Fargo was worried that Harragan and Tatum weren't there. After a couple of seconds, however, there was the sound of chair legs scraping the floor, and Harragan's voice came through the door.

"Who's there?"

"Angelique Leblanc."

"Angelique? What are you doing here?"

"I need to talk to you."

Harragan didn't respond, but Fargo thought he could hear him whispering to someone in the room.

"What about?"

"It's about Fargo. Marshal Tatum's got him locked in the jail. I'm afraid he might do something to him."

She was a good actress, Fargo thought. She even managed to get a little catch in her voice.

A key turned in the lock, and Angelique stepped down.

Fargo took her place. The door opened, but only a little way.

"Come around to the front," Harragan said. "I don't like to open this door after dark."

That was enough to let Fargo know that something was wrong. He pulled his .44, drew back his foot, and kicked the door, which flew open and hit someone in the room. Probably Harragan.

The door bounced back at Fargo, and before he could kick it again, someone fell against it and slammed it shut. The key turned in the lock again.

"Shit," Fargo said.

No use to worry about fooling anybody now. He kicked the door again. It didn't give. One more time, and the frame splintered around the lock. The door swung open, but there was no one inside the office. The door leading into the hotel was open.

"Shit," Fargo said again.

He ran through the room and into the hotel lobby. He looked around and saw only the startled desk clerk.

"Where did Harragan go?" he said.

The clerk hesitated. Fargo waved the pistol barrel in his direction, and he pointed to the front door. His voice quavered. "That way."

Fargo was out the door in an instant but he didn't see anyone. The dark street appeared deserted.

To the left, the street led back into town. To the right was the spring where Fargo and Angelique had relaxed and beyond that the woods and hills.

Harragan and Tatum had disappeared.

"Where are they, Skye?" Angelique said, coming up beside him.

"Gone," Fargo said.

"They couldn't be gone. They weren't that far ahead of us."

143

Fargo peered into the darkness around the spring. "Something moved over there. I'm going to have a look. You wait here."

"I'm coming with you."

"Not a good idea. Somebody has to wait here in case they try to come back."

Angelique opened her mouth, then shut it. "All right, but if you're not back in ten minutes, I'm coming after you."

Fargo didn't argue because it wouldn't have done any good. He nodded and headed for the spring.

A half-moon hung in the sky and gave a little light, but when Fargo arrived at the spring, he didn't see anything unusual. Nothing moved in the brush and trees nearby, and while Fargo could hear a few muffled sounds from the hotel and from town, the area around the spring was quiet.

Fargo stood still. He could stand that way for a long time if he had to, probably longer than whoever or whatever he'd seen. He waited.

A minute went by, then another. Something rustled in the bushes across from the spring. Fargo trained his pistol on the spot. The rustling stopped.

It could have been a raccoon, or maybe a bird, but Fargo didn't think so. He made his way around the rim of the spring, keeping a close eye on the bushes.

He was almost to the spot where he thought the rustling had been when he heard the scream. It came from back near the hotel and sounded a lot like Angelique.

Fargo turned away from the bushes, and as soon as he did Tatum burst out of them. He crossed the narrow strip of ground between him and Fargo before the Trailsman could make his turn. He hit Fargo hard, wrapping his long, thick arms around him. Fargo dropped his pistol just before Tatum drove him into the spring.

They hit the water together, and Tatum held Fargo gripped in a crushing embrace. Fargo hadn't had time to think about taking a deep breath, and he knew he'd soon be out of air. Tatum must have prepared himself before charging Fargo, and his plan would be simple: hold Fargo under until he drowned.

Tatum was bigger than Fargo, and he had a big advantage. Fargo was trapped in a bear hug. He couldn't maneuver. He didn't have his pistol, and he had no way to get to the Arkansas toothpick.

To make things even worse, Tatum was tightening his grip, crushing Fargo to him and squeezing out what little air Fargo had left in his lungs.

It was dark beneath the steaming water, but Fargo opened his eyes. He could barely make out the contours of Tatum's face above his, but he would have sworn that the marshal's mouth was twisted into a sadistic grin.

Fargo knew how it was supposed to turn out. He'd be the second drowning within a couple of days, but no one would care. He was, after all, an escaped prisoner. Tatum could have shot him, but he must have taken pleasure in a more personal kind of killing. Or maybe he was afraid he'd miss and not get a chance for a second shot. Whatever the reason, he had Fargo in serious danger of dying.

Fargo's lungs burned with the need for air. The Trailsman tried to twist, but he couldn't move at all. Tatum held him too tightly.

Fargo's attempt to move seemed to anger Tatum, who squeezed even harder, which Fargo wouldn't have thought was possible. Fargo thought the size of Tatum's grin increased, but he couldn't be sure.

Fargo remembered having been in a similar situation when the man had tried to strangle him in the bottom of Dave Harragan's grave. What worked then wouldn't work now because the water would slow down any blow Fargo could deliver with his head, and the distance between him and Tatum was so small that Fargo didn't think he could do any damage, anyway.

A feeling of great weariness crept over Fargo. It would be easy to give in, just let go, breathe in, and let his life slip away into the darkness of the water.

The heat of the water lulled him. Sleep. That's all it would amount to, just another kind of sleep. What could be wrong with that?

But enough of Fargo's will to live remained to remind him that the major problem with the kind of sleep he was contemplating was that there wouldn't be any waking up from it.

"Can't have that," Fargo said, or thought, but he still didn't know what he could do about it.

Well, maybe one thing. He raised his head up. He was almost as tall as Tatum, and the way that Tatum held him put Fargo's head about on a level with Tatum's neck.

Fargo didn't bother to look for a soft spot. He just clamped his teeth on to the first likely spot he could find and bit down as hard as he could.

Tatum flinched. Fargo shook his head like a dog shaking a rat it was trying to kill. He thought maybe he had a tendon in his mouth. He wondered if it was possible to tear it right out of Tatum's body. He didn't know, but he was sure as hell going to try.

Fargo tasted salty blood. It wasn't warm, or not as warm as the water they were in. Fargo shook his head and tried to make his teeth meet.

Bubbles burst from Tatum's mouth as he opened it in a silent scream, and the marshal let go of Fargo. As soon as he did, Fargo's hand went for the big knife in its sheath even as Fargo stood up.

The Trailsman's head burst out of the water. Steaming rivulets ran from his head and beard. He gasped for breath, smoothed back his hair, and wiped water out of his eyes with his free hand.

Across the pool, Tatum tried to pull himself out of the water. Fargo flipped the knife so that he held the blade. He took another deep breath, relishing the feel of the cool air as he sucked it in. Without thinking much about his target, he threw the knife.

The knife spun end over end, and the blade sank deep into the back of Tatum's thigh.

The marshal pitched forward onto the ground, halfway out of the spring. Fargo sloshed through the water after him. Tatum tried to turn over, but Fargo reached him before he could do it.

Fargo took the handle of his knife and pulled it free. Tatum tried to squirm away. Fargo grabbed his belt and pulled him back into the spring. Blood poured from the marshal's neck. Fargo shoved him away, and Tatum fell backward with a splash.

"Sink or swim," Fargo said. "Doesn't matter to me, one way or the other."

The Trailsman got out of the spring and located his pistol. His buckskins stuck to him like another skin, but he didn't have time to worry about that.

He started back to the hotel at a run.

12

Fargo thought he must have looked like some kind of freshly caught fish with his clammy clothing stuck to him as he burst through the front door of the hotel, but there were no guests to see him. The lobby was clear except for the desk clerk.

The clerk's eyes bugged when he saw the Trailsman hurrying toward him. Water still dripped from his clothes.

"No time for foolishness," Fargo said, brandishing the Arkansas toothpick at him. "You're either going to tell me the truth about where Harragan is, or I'm going to slit you from asshole to appetite."

To emphasize that he wasn't joking, Fargo leaned over the counter and stuck the point of the big knife into the clerk's belly. The man's eyes crossed as a spot of blood appeared on his shirt.

Fargo jiggled the toothpick. "I'll count to five. No, I'll count to three. One, two—"

"Don't!" the clerk said. His voice was an octave or so higher than the last time he'd spoken to Fargo. "Don't! He's in the office! He's in the office!"

Maybe he was, and maybe he wasn't. Fargo remembered that back door. He put his knife away and pulled the .44.

The office door was locked. Fargo kicked it once, water squishing from his boot, and the door snapped backward.

The office was vacant. Fargo went to the back door, but he didn't open it. He didn't like the idea of framing himself in the lighted doorway or stepping out into the darkness. Harragan could be anywhere out there. Fargo opened the door a tiny crack and listened. He hoped that if Angelique were able, she'd let him know where she was by making some kind of sound, but Fargo heard nothing.

Not from outside.

But noise came from under the desk. The drumming of heels and someone making squeaking noises. Harragan could have been hiding there, but Fargo didn't think it was likely. He took a cautious peek and saw Angelique, her hands and feet tied with strips of her own shirt. What was left over was stuffed in her mouth. Fargo pulled it out.

"Where's Harragan?"

"He went out the back. He's on his way to kill Clyde and Prudence."

Fargo slipped out the Arkansas toothpick and slit the cloth that bound Angelique.

"Why?" he said.

"Prudence came here and told him that you were onto him. That she'd convinced you he was behind everything. That's why Harragan had you arrested. He and Tatum are working together, all right." She paused. "Is what she said true? Is she the one who convinced you?"

"No. I wasn't convinced. She must have convinced herself of it."

Fargo helped Angelique from beneath the desk.

"I think he was going to kill me, too," she said, "but he

changed his mind." She looked at Fargo carefully for the first time. "You're soaked. What happened?"

"Not now. I need to stop Harragan."

"You were right about him. Look." Angelique pointed to the desktop where Harragan's eye patch lay. "His eye is perfectly fine."

Fargo didn't have time for any more conversation.

"Stay here," he said, and left through the back door of the office.

He didn't look behind him, but he knew Angelique was back there even if she didn't have a shirt on. She never listened to anybody.

Fargo smelled smoke almost as soon as he was out the door, and when he got to the street, he saw that the Superior Hotel was on fire.

The blaze, which appeared to be on the second floor, wasn't big yet, but it soon would be. Someone started to ring the fire bell, but Fargo knew the town wouldn't have much in the way of a fire department.

People were pouring out of the hotel. The blaze leapt higher, and Fargo tried to make out the features of the fleeing people. He didn't see Prudence or Clyde. Or Harragan. He'd have to go inside.

Someone pulled on his wet buckskins.

"No, Skye," Angelique said from behind him.

"I have to," Fargo said.

He pulled away from her and ran across the street and into the burning building. The fire wasn't serious yet, but the smoke was black and billowing. The smoke, not the fire, was the real danger.

Well, it wasn't just the smoke, Fargo thought. Since the fire was above him, the building might collapse on top of him. That would be more dangerous than the smoke.

He tried to consider Harragan's thinking. Burning

the hotel might have been enough revenge for him, but leaving Brundage and Prudence trapped inside would be even better. But where would he leave them?

Not on the second floor. Brundage hadn't been feeling well and would have been hard to get upstairs. The easiest thing to do would be to leave him in his room and hope he and Prudence died from inhaling smoke or from falling timbers. That would also give them time to think about dying, and Harragan might have liked that idea, too.

He knew the way to Clyde's room, and though he could hardly see, he went in that direction, trying not to breathe too deeply. Even at that the smoke seared his nose and throat, the feeling made worse because of his recent underwater struggles with Tatum.

Fargo pulled off his still-damp bandanna and tied it over his mouth and nose. It helped a little. He looked like a road agent, but he didn't think anyone who happened to see him would care.

He bumped into the counter, felt his way around it, and found the door to Brundage's office. The flames crackled and spit above him, and cinders drifted down. He could hear the dim cries from outside as the bucket brigade tried to douse the flames, but there wasn't any way for them to get the water to the second floor, another good reason to start the fire there.

The doorknob was hot, but the door swung open, and Fargo went through the office to the door into Brundage's room.

Fargo didn't know what he'd do if Clyde and Prudence weren't there.

Leave, he told himself. If they weren't there, there wouldn't be anything he could do.

He opened the door. Smoke billowed out.

"Prudence?" he said. "Brundage?"

The only answer he got was a cough from the direction of the bed. He crossed the room, banging his shin on a chair. He took hold of the chair and pushed it in front of him.

When he got to the bed, he could make out the forms of two figures on it. He ran his hands over the nearest. A man. Brundage, probably, tied with cloth ripped from the sheets.

Fargo cut the cloth with his knife, then freed Prudence. That done, he smashed out the window with the chair. Cool air rushed into the room.

He helped Prudence sit up. "Can you walk?" he said.

Her answer was a cough, so Fargo helped her off the bed and to the window. He knew she wouldn't be able to climb out, so he lifted her through, then held her wrists and let her down to the ground.

Brundage was in even worse shape, but Fargo got him to the window and out through it. When Brundage was on the ground, Fargo went through the window, too.

Prudence sat on the ground nearby.

"Come on," Fargo said, helping her to her feet. He tore the bandanna off his face. "We have to get away from here."

"I'll help her, Skye."

It was Angelique again. Fargo had thought she might follow him into the building, but she'd been too smart for that. She'd known where he might show up, and here she was.

"Get her to the street," Fargo said. "I'll bring Brundage."

He picked Brundage up and threw him over his back like a sack of grain. Angelique was already halfway out the alley, but Fargo caught up with her.

"I don't guess you saw Harragan," he said.

"No," Angelique said with a shake of her head.

"Any idea where he might have gone?"

"Maybe to burn down another building," Angelique said.

Fargo dumped Brundage across the street from what was left of his hotel, and Angelique left Prudence sitting beside him. Fargo didn't think either of them was fully aware of what was happening in front of them, and that was probably just as well. What mattered now was finding Harragan.

Angelique was probably right. Harragan would complete his revenge somehow. That was why he hadn't killed Angelique. It wasn't because of any love he had for her. He'd wanted to be sure she was around to know he'd destroyed her saloon. He wouldn't have been worried about Fargo. He must have thought that Fargo was dead, taken care of by Tatum, so with both Fargo and Angelique out of the way, he could take his time with the Traveler.

"It's not burning yet," Angelique said as they approached the saloon.

"Could be he decided to get out of town," Fargo said, knowing even as he spoke that Harragan wouldn't have done that.

"What do we do?" Angelique said.

Fargo stopped and thought about it. Harragan was alone. If he was smart, he wouldn't have gone to the Traveler until everyone had left to see the fire at the Superior.

"Did you see anybody from the saloon at the fire?" Fargo said.

"I wasn't looking for them. I think I caught a glimpse of Rose and the girls."

"What about Albert or Sam?"

"I didn't see either of them."

Fargo didn't think the two men would have been

able to overpower Harragan, especially if Harragan was armed. They might both be dead by now.

Maybe not, though. Albert might not like fighting, but he wasn't a coward. He hadn't hesitated to follow Fargo to the jail when Tatum arrested him. Neither had Sam.

"You count to a hundred," Fargo told Angelique. "Then go in the door. I'm going around to the back."

"That didn't work out so well the last time you tried it."

Fargo had to grin. She was right.

"I appreciate the reminder. Start counting."

"One," Angelique said, and Fargo was off.

He counted, too, and he reached the back door of the saloon long before he got to a hundred. He kept counting and wondered if Angelique was counting faster or slower then he was. He also wondered if Harragan was inside. And if he was, had he blocked the door?

Fargo strained his ears, hoping to hear something from the saloon that would give him a clue as to what was happening in there. He heard nothing until after his counting reached a hundred and twelve. Then he heard Angelique's voice.

"Harragan!"

At the muffled reply, Fargo drew his .44, opened the door, and went into the Traveler.

Harragan sat at the piano, his pistol in his hand. Across from him on the bar sat Albert and Sam. Their hands were trapped beneath their thighs. Angelique stood in the doorway.

"Come on in," Harragan said to her. "I've been waiting for you. You can come in, too, Fargo. Just lay your gun on the floor unless you want me to start shooting."

Fargo thought it over. He could shoot Harragan, but Harragan might still get off a shot or two. No telling who he'd hit, though his pistol was pointed at Angelique. If

Fargo missed, which was possible though not likely, or if he didn't kill Harragan with the first shot, things would get messy.

"I'm sorry, Miss Leblanc," Albert said. "He came in as everybody was going to the fire. We didn't even know him without the eye patch."

"He doesn't look any better," Angelique said.

He did look a lot different, however. Fargo wasn't sure he'd have recognized him if they'd passed in the street at night. Daytime might have been different.

"The pistol, Fargo," Harragan said.

Fargo laid the .44 on the floor.

"Slide it over here," Harragan said while Fargo was bent over.

Fargo slid the gun in Harragan's direction.

"That's good," Harragan said. "Now just stay where you are while I decide what to do."

It was quiet in the saloon. Fargo could hear the noise of the crowd still gathered at the Superior. They wouldn't be there much longer, and most of them would be thirsty after the fire. He wondered how long he could stall Harragan.

Harragan must have been thinking along the same lines.

"I won't be here long," he said. "I decided not to burn this place down because I wanted to see Fargo again. You ruined a good setup for me, Fargo. I was trying to settle down and be an upstanding citizen, and you just wouldn't let me."

"Right," Fargo said. "Just another honest man trying to earn a living by running everybody else out of business."

"I guess that's one way of looking at it. Doesn't matter now. I wanted to see you, too, Angelique. You should've married me when you had the chance."

"I'd as soon marry a frog."

"Too bad for you then. You and Fargo made this personal for me. Now I'll just have to kill you both."

"Do it, then."

"Full of gumption right to the end," Harragan said. "I like that. But I think I'll kill Albert first."

He pulled the trigger of his pistol. The noise of the shot filled the room, and Albert tumbled backward, falling behind the bar.

Fargo's hand went down for the Arkansas toothpick.

"Don't try it, Fargo," said Tatum, as he came through the door and shoved Angelique to the floor.

The side of his neck looked as if a wolf had chewed it, and he was none too steady on his feet. The pistol in his hand was steady enough, however.

"What the hell happened to you?" Harragan said.

"Fargo," Tatum said. "I'm going to kill him."

Fargo had never expected to see Tatum again. He'd thought Tatum was either dead or would drown. The big man had been stronger than Fargo had thought.

"I was planning to do that myself," Harragan said. "But you go on ahead."

Tatum pulled the trigger of his pistol.

Nothing happened.

Wet powder, Fargo thought. He'd expected it. The swim in the spring hadn't done the pistol's loads any good.

"Shit," Tatum said.

That was the last thing he ever said. Albert rose up from behind the bar, his shirt blood-soaked, and triggered a shotgun blast that ripped Tatum's upper body apart. Albert dropped the shotgun and clung to the bar.

Fargo had caught sight of Albert just before the shot, so he'd been ready. While Harragan was distracted, Fargo brought out his knife and sent it on its way. It sliced through the air and buried itself up to the hilt in Harragan's neck. Blood spurted, and Harragan toppled off the chair, firing a shot into the ceiling as he fell.

He hit the floor and pawed at the handle of the knife buried in his throat. Then his hands fell away from it, he twitched a time or two, and that was all.

"Thanks, Albert," Fargo said. "I thought you didn't like fighting."

"I don't," Albert said.

He let go of the bar and sank back down behind the it again.

"I'll get the doctor," Sam said, hopping down from the bar.

"Better see if you can find Corby Carson, too," Fargo said as Sam ran out. "Tell him we have some more customers for him."

Angelique stood up. "I know he'll be glad to hear that. I could use a drink, Skye. How about you?"

"Sounds like a fine idea," Fargo said.

As Fargo had expected, there wasn't much left of the Superior Hotel, but both Prudence and Clyde Brundage recovered quickly. Albert didn't do as well, but the doctor said he'd be fine in a week or so, though he wouldn't have much use of his arm for a while. The kick of the shotgun hadn't helped any.

"I think Clyde likes you again," Fargo told Angelique a couple of days later as they sat listening to Sam play "Hard Times Come Again No More" on the piano.

Angelique smiled. "Prudence told him how I helped rescue them. He's decided that I'm not so bad, after all. Prudence likes me, too." She paused. "Is there anything you'd like to tell me about her, Skye?"

"Can't think of a thing," Fargo said, taking a sip of coffee.

"You want some more of that?" Corby Carson called from the bar. "I got half a pot left."

"I'm fine," Fargo said.

Carson had taken over as temporary bartender while Albert was on the mend. He said he could handle it because he wouldn't have any business at his place for a while. "No more folks left for Fargo to kill," was the way he'd put it.

"You think Brundage will take over the Grand Hotel?" Fargo said.

"I do," Angelique said. "I'm not sure how complicated it will be, but I don't imagine Harragan left any heirs, and he bought the place with stolen money to begin with. It might be complicated, but Clyde wants to do it. So he will."

"You think he'll try to pressure you into marrying him?"

Angelique smiled an innocent smile. "He won't have to pressure me."

"I didn't think he would."

"He's not up to asking me yet," Angelique said. "Are you sure you have to leave town now?"

Fargo nodded. "I'm sure. Been here too long already. I need to get back on the trail. Besides, Brundage wouldn't like it if I stayed."

"Prudence might."

Fargo grinned. "You never can tell."

He stood up, picked up his hat from the table, and settled it on his head. He bent over and gave Angelique a quick good-bye kiss.

"Hey, Sam," he said as he straightened up. "Can you play 'The Arkansas Traveler'?"

"Sure can," Sam said, and the lively strains of the tune followed the Trailsman out the door.

LOOKING FORWARD!

**The following is the opening
section of the next novel in the exciting
Trailsman series from Signet:**

TRAILSMAN #347
DAKOTA DEATH TRAP

*The Dakotas, 1861—the Trailsman is
caught in a web of deceit.*

The Sioux had been after Skye Fargo for five days.

A small fire was to blame. He had kindled it in a dry
wash to roast a grouse. The evening sky had been clear,
not a cloud in sight, which was why the gust of wind
out of nowhere caught him by surprise. The next he
knew, the flames leapt to a patch of grass and crackled
to the top of the wash. He stomped most of the flames
out and threw dirt on the rest but the harm had been
done.

Fargo scanned the prairie and spotted riders on a low
hill a quarter of a mile away. That they were warriors was
obvious, and since he was in the heart of Sioux country,
it wasn't hard to guess which tribe. He had a few friends
among the Sioux; he had lived with a band once. But
since of late the Sioux had been helping themselves to
the hair of every white they came across, he'd rolled up

his blankets and saddled the Ovaro and gotten the hell out of there.

No sooner did he burst out of the wash than war whoops rent the air and arrows buzzed like angry hornets. Fargo used his spurs and left the warriors breathing the stallion's dust. He'd figured that was the end of it. They couldn't track in the dark. He rode all night to be safe, only to discover, to his shock, that he wasn't. At first light there they were, half a mile back. One of them had to be a damn good tracker.

For five days Fargo pushed to the southeast. For five days they doggedly stuck to his trail. He could have ambushed them. Find a spot and lie in wait and when they came in range, pick off as many as he could with his Henry. With a full tube and one in the chamber, the rifle held sixteen rounds. He was a marksman; he could drop half the war party before they collected their wits. But he kept on riding. He had made a pact with himself that he never killed unless he had to. Usually.

It was the middle of the morning on the sixth day when Fargo looked back and saw that the Sioux were no longer following him. They had turned around and were heading to the northwest, back into the heart of their territory. He drew rein and watched until they were out of sight. He wondered if it was a trick but he couldn't see how. He had too large a lead for them to circle around and lie in wait somewhere up ahead.

"I reckon they decided I wasn't worth the bother," Fargo summed up his thoughts out loud.

Before him rose green hills. He wound in among them and came on a stream. Climbing down at a shallow pool, he sank to a knee, dipped his hand in the water, and sipped. "Fit to drink," he announced, and let the stallion lower its muzzle.

Fargo could see his reflection. His buckskins were speckled with dust and his once-white hat was practically brown. His red bandanna hung loose and could use re-tying. His blue eyes were a deeper blue than the water and his beard could use a trim. He went to dip his hand in again when the brush on the other side rustled and a horse snorted. Instantly, he swooped his right hand to his Colt. But he didn't draw.

Out of the brush came a woman tugging on the reins to a bay. Her back was to Fargo and she hadn't noticed him yet. All he saw was a black dress and a black shawl and a wealth of curly black hair. The bay was limping.

"Need some help there, ma'am?"

The woman spun. Fear froze her rigid and she blurted, "Oh! I didn't know you were there."

Now that Fargo could see the rest of her, he liked what he saw. She had lovely emerald eyes and full red lips that reminded him of ripe raspberries. Her dress was doing all it could to contain a pair of watermelons. And her legs, if the way the dress clung to them was any hint, went on forever. Unfurling, he smiled and said, "I didn't mean to startle you."

She looked back the way she had come. "They're still after me."

"Ma'am?"

"They're after me," she said again. "You'd best hide. I won't tell them I saw you."

"Who is after you?"

She turned. "Please," she said, her concern for his welfare genuine. "You don't know what they're like. They might think you're helping me and pistol-whip you. Or they might do it for the fun of it." She motioned up the stream. "Run while you still can."

Fargo gathered she was in some sort of trouble and some hard cases were after her. It was none of his affair, but then again, she was nice on the eyes. "I'm not going anywhere."

"You really must," the woman pleaded. "I don't want you hurt on my account."

Before Fargo could ask her to elaborate, the woods pealed to the drum of galloping hooves and five riders swept down on her. They were stamped from the same mold: hard-faced, cold-eyed men, wearing enough hardware for an armory. They were so intent on her that they didn't spot him until they came to a stop. A stocky block of flab in a short-brimmed brown hat with a tear in the brim thrust out a thick finger and bellowed.

"Who's that yonder?"

The woman had swung the bay so it was between her and the riders. She said, "You leave him be, Sharpton. I don't know him."

Sharpton had two chins and a bulbous nose. He wore a Beaumont Adams revolver on his left side, butt forward for a cross draw. When he lowered his hand, he placed it on his belt an inch from the six-gun. "Who are you, mister?" he demanded. "And what the hell are you doing here?"

Fargo had been taking the measure of the others. Three were run-of-the mill frontier toughs. The last man, though, was different from the rest; he was tall—almost as tall as Fargo—and thin, and wore a black vest and a black hat and had a Smith & Wesson with walnut grips in a black leather holster high on his right hip. The man met Fargo's gaze, and nodded.

"Didn't you hear me?" Sharpton snapped.

"How could I not hear a big bag of wind like you?" Fargo answered, and stepped to the right so he was clear of the Ovaro.

"I asked you who you are," Sharpton said. "And I want to know what you're doing with this woman."

"I guess your pa never told you," Fargo said.

Sharpton blinked in confusion. "Eh?"

"That it's not smart to go around poking your big nose where it doesn't belong."

The rider in the black hat and vest chuckled.

"That's enough out of you, Blakely," Sharpton said.

"Oh?"

The man in the black hat and vest said it casually yet the effect it produced was instructive. The other three glanced at him and at Sharpton and reined their mounts to either side. As for Sharpton, his two chins bobbed and he quickly said, "I didn't mean nothing by that."

"Oh?" Blakely said again in that casual way of his.

"Damn it," Sharpton said. He had broken out in a sweat. "This is no time for you to be contrary. You want me to say I'm sorry? I'm sorry. Now can we get down to business and do what Mr. Mitchell told us to do." He turned to the woman. "Mount up, Honeydew. We're to escort you a good long way and make sure you don't come back."

"Honeydew?" Fargo grinned.

"My last name. My first name is Jasmine."

Sharpton gigged his horse closer to hers. "I won't say it again. Get on. You're leaving and you're leaving now."

"What if I refuse?" Jasmine said.

"You're going anyway."

Fargo took another step. "No," he said. "She's not."

They looked at him, the five of them, four grimly serious. Blakely seemed more amused than anything. Sharpton glanced at the Colt in Fargo's holster and then stared at Fargo's face and uncertainty crept into his own.

"You don't want to buck us on this."

Fargo didn't respond.

"You have any idea who we work for, mister? Abe Mitchell."

"The handle means nothing to me."

"It should. He's got a small army of gun hands working for him and we all do as he says."

"Good for him."

Sharpton scowled and shifted in his saddle. "You're not getting my point. Bucking us is dumb. It could get you killed."

"You are welcome to try," Fargo said. "Or do you talk a man to death to get up the gumption?"

Blakely laughed.

As for Sharpton, he turned red in the face and his fingers clenched and unclenched. "You think I won't?"

"I think you're a yellow streak who only tries when he has an edge," Fargo said. "Now either jerk that smoke wagon or get the hell out of here before I lose my temper."

Sharpton hauled on his reins and wheeled his mount. Glaring over his shoulder, he snarled, "This ain't over. We'll meet again. The only reason I don't do it now is that we're not to shoot anyone without Mr. Mitchell's say-so."

"Whatever excuse helps you sleep," Fargo said.

Sharpton used his spurs and the rest did the same except for Blakely who touched his hat brim to Honeydew and grinned at Fargo. "I should pay you for the entertainment. Watch your back if you drift into Hapgood Pond." He lifted the reins to go.

"Why are you riding with trash like Sharpton?" Fargo asked.

Blakely paused. "I thank you for the compliment." He sighed and gazed after the departing riders. "I have no control over who else Mr. Mitchell hires to protect him."

"So it's just the money."

"A man does what he has to to put food in his belly." Again Blakely lifted the reins.

"You don't mind the sour taste in your mouth?"

Blakely's features hardened slightly. "You're dangerous, friend. I hope it doesn't come down to you and me. I'd hate to have to kill someone with your fine sense of humor." He nodded at Jasmine and calmly rode off at a walk.

"A strange man," Jasmine said quietly.

Fargo turned to her.

"He rides with those gun sharks but he's nothing like them," Jasmine said. "He's always polite to women, for one thing. And he talks better, for another. Yet they say he's the deadliest of all of them. They say he's so fast, you don't see his hand move when he draws."

"That's fast." Fargo could recall more than a few instances when the same had been said about him. "But let's talk about you." He gave her his most charming smile and ran his eyes from her lustrous hair to the tips of her small shoes. "God was nice to me today."

"You have hungry eyes, sir," Jasmine said.

"I haven't been with a woman in over a week."

"That long?" Jasmine smirked. "But you're right. God has been nice to both of us. More so than you can imagine." With that, she reached up and removed her shawl. Her dress was topped by a white collar that went completely around her neck.

"What the hell?" Fargo said. The last time he had seen a collar like that had been on a parson.

"I didn't fully introduce myself. I am *Reverend* Honeydew, a duly ordained minister. And I am pleased to meet you, my brother." She came over and held out her hand for him to shake.

"Brother?" Fargo repeated.

"We are all brothers and sisters in the eyes of the Lord."

"Son of a bitch," Fargo said.

"Now, now. I'll thank you not to curse in my presence, if you don't mind." Jasmine replaced her shawl and smoothed her dress, her watermelons jiggling with every movement.

Fargo sighed and turned to the Ovaro and gripped the saddle horn. "Be seeing you, ma'am."

"Hold on. Where are you going?"

"I'm heading east. I have to meet a man in Saint Louis at the end of the month about guiding a wagon train." Fargo went to hike his leg.

"No. Please. You can't leave."

"Why not?" Fargo had done his good deed for the year and had no hankering to stick around. She was an eyeful but getting her out of that dress would take more time and effort than he had to spare.

"You're an answer to my prayers."

"You're loco." Once more Fargo raised his boot.

"Please. Hear me out." Jasmine clasped her hands to her more than ample bosom. "Hapgood Pond is dearly in need of a shepherd. There are saloons and fallen doves. And where you have drink and tarts you have sinners."

Fargo thought of all the doves he had been with, but kept it to himself.

"For some reason, Abe Mitchell doesn't like outsiders," Jasmine had gone on. "I was told that his men have run a number of travelers off. Sharpton was doing the same to me when I stumbled on you."

"What the hell harm can a preacher do?"

"I think Sharpton got carried away. I hadn't been in Hapgood Pond an hour when he showed up and began badgering me with questions. When I didn't answer to his satisfaction, he pushed me and told me to get out. He said that if I didn't, he would do things to me." She stopped and blushed. "You can imagine what kind of things. Anyway, he marched me to my horse and made me ride off. I yelled at him that I would be back, and that's when he and the others came after me."

"Running off strangers is peculiar."

"Isn't it though? So there I was, in desperate straits, and out of the blue you showed up. Do you see what that means?"

"I am a flame and good-looking women are the moths."

"What? No. Why would you say a thing like that?" Jasmine shook her head. "This was divine design. God sent you to help me."

"Oh, hell," Fargo said.

"Return with me to Hapgood Pond and see that I am not run off a second time."

Fargo thought of the saloons and the doves, especially the doves. "Preacher lady, lead the way."

No other series packs this much heat!

THE TRAILSMAN

Follow the trail of Penguin's Action Westerns at
penguin.com/actionwesterns